HARRY KENMARE, PI
AT YOUR SERVICE

SHORT STORIES

A. B. PATTERSON

Also by A. B. Patterson

Novels:

Harry's World
© 2015

Harry's Quest
© 2018

Harry Kenmare short stories:
(Second edition versions included in this volume)

'Little Rich Street Girl'
(First published in *Switchblade* – Issue
#3 – Special Edition   © 2017)

'White Powder, Black leather, Grey Badges'
(First published in *Switchblade* – Issue # 4   © 2018)

'Wankers'
(First published in *Switchblade* – Issue # 8   © 2019)

Other short stories:

'Blue Angel'
(Published in *Econoclash Review* – Issue # 4   © 2019)

HARRY KENMARE, PI
AT YOUR SERVICE

Published by A. B. Patterson 2020
PO Box 1008
Broadway
NSW 2007
Australia

First Printing 2020

Cover design by J.T.Lindroos
www.jtlindroos.carbonmade.com
Cover photographs from © iStock and © A. B. Patterson
Interior artwork by Ran Scott
Twitter @RSPMystery
Logo design by Stephen Hill at Dylunio

 A catalogue record for this book is available from the National Library of Australia

ISBN: 978-0-9923273-4-7 (paperback)

Also available as an ebook:
ISBN: 978-0-9923273-5-4

Published with the assistance of Publicious Book Publishing
www.publicious.com.au

To freedom of expression …
… and all its brave voices.

Contents

About the Author

A. B. Patterson is an Australian writer who knows first-hand about corruption, power, crime and sex. He was a Detective Sergeant in the WA Police, working in paedophilia and vice, and later a Chief Investigator with the NSW Independent Commission Against Corruption.

His multiple award-winning, debut novel, *Harry's World*, introduced the jaded and flawed PI Harry Kenmare. *Harry's Quest* was the sizzling, award-winning sequel in the

PI Harry Kenmare series of novels. The third novel, *Harry's Grail*, is in progress.

His Harry Kenmare short stories, some previously published in the USA in *Switchblade* magazine, are gathered together here for the first time.

His hard-boiled, gritty, and noir writing style has been likened to that of Raymond Chandler and Ken Bruen.

He makes no apologies for telling it how it is.

C'est la vie.

www.abpatterson.com.au

Author's Foreword

I was introduced, as a much younger reader, to the short story form by way of the works of W. Somerset Maugham, who remains to this day one of my favourite English writers. What he could achieve in a limited word count was truly awe-inspiring. And whilst I love a good novel, or novella, the short story form has always grabbed me with its ability, in the right hands, to deliver a great story in the juiciest of morsels.

My first novel, *Harry's World*, began its life as a draft short story, although it rapidly morphed into the novel that now exists. My real introduction into deliberately writing short stories came a little later, courtesy of the wonderful anthology of hard-boiled and noir crime stories, *Switchblade* magazine out of Los Angeles. I was fortunate enough to happen upon *Switchblade* just as it started up, and was immediately hooked on the power of the short fiction that steamed from its pages. I read the first two issues, got pumped up, and thought I'd give a submission a fly.

So, the first Harry short story was born, 'Little Rich Street Girl', landing on the pages of *Switchblade* in 2017. And it's apt for that story to open this volume. I'd also decided to try writing Harry from a first person point of view, which turned out to be an entirely different experience from the third person the novels are written in. And it's been huge fun, might I say. As history shows, the editor of *Switchblade*, the illustrious Scotch Rutherford, liked my work enough to give it a run. And two further stories have followed in the *Switchblade* issues, so far. I will forever be in the debt of Mr Rutherford for the motivation and encouragement that flowed from his acceptance of my work.

Writing short stories is now an integral part of my work as an author, alongside the novels. The short, sharp impact of a well-crafted short story is a thing of beauty. I read more of them now than ever, and I love writing them.

I do hope the tales in this collection give you, my readers, a savagely tantalizing tingle of the taste buds as you chew on the spicy offerings to follow.

Please enjoy!

Cheers,

Andrew

A. B. Patterson

Sydney, February 2020

It's time to meet …

Harry Kenmare, PI

Harry Kenmare, PI

G'day, I'm Harry. Harry Kenmare, Private Investigator. I used to be a cop, detective sergeant. Until I got the arse for belting a rock spider. A child molester to most of you. Well, of course I belted the prick. I'd just lost my daughter, Orla, to scum like him. Orla was raped and murdered, by paedophile animals. And, being only human, that has shaped me as a man since then. You got a problem with that? Guess what, here's fifty cents, go call someone who cares.

Orla's mother, my very ex-wife, left at the same time. Decided her yoga instructor was more 'sensitive' to her needs. He was a pretentious arse-wipe, but he had inherited money. Yeah, so I married shallow, as it turns out. Not the first bloke down that baited burrow. And then she shagged a couple of other detectives. Sure it was to spite me. Rooting another detective's missus was a no-no, totally against the brotherhood's Code. Anyway, the arse-wipe yoga instructor got done for dealing 'herbal remedies', went to prison, and the ex became his ex, too. Some degree of karma, maybe. No doubt she's off now making some other poor bastard's life an abject misery.

Anyhow, my motto now is: 'Here for a good time, not a long time'. And I live by it. I smoke, I drink like a fish, I eat rich food, and I bed every good sort I can charm back to my apartment. I love the ladies. I'm what in days gone by was described as a libertine. And if you've got a problem with that, hear this: I don't give a flying rat's arse.

Enough of my loves. What about the other side of the ledger? I hate injustice, I hate hypocrisy, I hate misogyny, I hate bullies, and I hate the Establishment. A long list. No shortage of candidates in Sydney. And wherever I can deliver karma, I'll do so in spades.

You might love me, or you might hate me. But you'll never forget me.

Cheers,
Harry

– Case #1 –

LITTLE RICH STREET GIRL

She had one of those lovely model faces that shouted Fresh, Clean and Cheerful, that sells toothpaste or gives head with the same wooden sincerity.

- James Crumley

LITTLE RICH STREET GIRL

– 1 –

Coagulating semen clung to the lock of grubby, blonde hair dangling next to her cheek. Obviously not all of a previous load had gone down her throat. I guessed she wasn't concerned about the finer points of her appearance. On these seedy streets, appearances were shallow, skanky, and purely commercial. It was about semen and cash, giving and receiving. Prices depended on the delivery context: oral, vaginal, or anal; condom or bareback (for the true fatalists); and how desperate the girl was for her next hit.

I figured Smokey, as she introduced herself, had got fixed up in the last couple of hours, judging by the languid way she flopped herself into the front seat of my hire-car, and the slightly heavy-lidded look to her bright blue eyes. Not even the opiates could erase their natural sparkle.

She gave me a lazy, lopsided smile, unabashedly slid her hand into my crotch, and looked me in the eye.

'So, what would handsome like today?'

Sexy voice. That, married with her hand gently kneading my tackle, got some distinct movement. She detected it. Well, it was her job.

'Handsome here likes what he sees then.' A statement, not a question.

My cock had neither eyes nor common sense, but I'm no orphan there in the male world.

'You got me,' I smiled. 'What's on offer, sexy babe?'

'What's your name?'

'They call me Harry.'

Actually, that is my name. I've been called a lot of other things along the way. Things your mother would wash your mouth out with soap for saying. If your mother was a washing kind of lady, that is.

Smokey's hand tightened on my balls. She tried to look serious.

'You're not a pig are you?'

Well, I'm not. Used to be, years ago. Now I'm a hard-drinking PI, scrapping around for work, and living as hedonistically as possible, cash reserves allowing. After all, life's short, play hard. A motto I've always liked. Another one is that attack is the best form of defence. So, I responded to the inquisitorial clutching of my balls by grabbing one of her breasts, squeezing hard, and doing a much better severe impersonation.

'No, I'm fucking not. Are you?'

She wasn't ready for the counter-attack: mental reflexes too slow. She headed back to familiar territory, regaining the come-fuck-me smile and putting enough tongue along her lips to make a bishop bar up.

'It's your eyes,' she murmured. 'They've got a copper's look to them.'

Yeah, not much I could do about that. Ex-coppers always have a certain vigilance to their eyes, it's true. Smokey had picked up some street smarts all right, as young as she was. Thought I'd throw her a bone, figuratively speaking you understand.

'Well spotted. Long time ago. Now I'm a private detective.'

She nodded slowly.

'Cool. And what would Mr Private Detective like to do with his cock today?'

'What's on the menu, sexy?' I kept my hand on her breast, but gently now. She seemed to like it.

'Fifty for head. Hundred for straight. Extra fifty for anal. Double it up for bareback.'

I looked at her hand rubbing my crotch, then up her arm to the fresh track marks. Bareback? You kidding? You'd have to be on a serious death-wish to do anything out here without a rubber.

'That's quite a menu,' I said, smiling at her.

She'd got me as hard as a rock and it had been a while since I last drained the lizard. What was a man to do?

– **2** –

Three days earlier in Sydney had been a disgustingly humid November day. I was sitting in my steamy, run-down office, air-con stuffed again, and the tight-arsed landlord not returning seventeen messages. I'd hold back the next rent. That'd guarantee a call.

The phone did ring, but it wasn't to fix the temperature. It was some personal assistant, Lionel something. But his boss's name I knew: Marcus Standing, property developer and Sydney A-Lister, address in Point Piper. Where else with that sort of money? The most expensive suburb in the second most expensive city on Planet Earth.

Apparently I had an excellent reputation for tracking people down, so Lionel had heard. Mr Standing, it transpired, had need of my services. I was to 'report', no less, to his harbourside palace at 9 a.m. tomorrow morning. Shit, I'd even have to break out a decent suit for the occasion. Luckily I kept one in the wardrobe, permanently in its plastic sheath from the dry-cleaners. And double shit, I'd be best off to go easy on the grog tonight. Bloody work.

At 0845 hours, in my language, I pulled up to the large, bronze gate of the modest Standing abode: eleven bedrooms and six bathrooms, according to the Internet. And who the fuck needs six bathrooms? Can their cooking really be that bad?

I pressed the intercom and announced myself, wondering if I'd be directed to a tradesman's entrance instead.

Standing was worth about two billion dollars, and did a lot of his business out of London, alternating between the two hemispheres to squeeze in two summers a year. Hard life. He had married into English aristocracy: Lady Ophelia Montague-Forsythe, who looked pretty hot in her media photos. There were two daughters.

The gate opened in a well-oiled glide. A hard-looking fucker in a suit with a bulging armpit stood at the side of the driveway. I stopped next to him: his hand instructed it. With his arsenal of commanding charisma, he had to be ex-military, probably special forces.

You don't fuck with these types. And, believe me, you don't try humour either. They don't have any. It gets removed from their personalities in the very first week of training, somewhere between the lesson on looking stern and dangerous, and the workshop on shoving sharp steel blades into carotid arteries.

'Harry Kenmare, I'm expected.'

The iceman looked at me and held out his hand. Not for shaking.

'ID, please.'

I pulled out my PI licence and put it into his deeply scarred palm. Looked nasty: as if he had rappelled down barbed wire. Probably used it afterwards to floss. As I said, you don't fuck with these guys.

He perused my ID, looked at me doing his best impersonation of Clint Eastwood with a migraine, and handed it back.

'Okay, Mr Kenmare. Park over next to the garden gate.'

'Thanks, mate.'

His eyes said being mates with me was about as likely as finding integrity in Parliament. Still, I wasn't shedding my Aussie vernacular for anyone.

I drove slowly up the paved driveway and parked precisely where directed.

As I wandered along the front terrace to the faux Corinthian portico, the solid, mahogany front door opened. A smiling butler stood inside. He was straight out of an E.M. Forster novel.

'Good morning, sir. Please do come in.'

I stepped over the threshold and looked around the elegant hallway. Marble, brass, and polished timber abounded. I inhaled deeply. The atmosphere was what I imagined lying in a swimming pool of used banknotes would be like.

'Please, come this way, sir.'

I followed him down the hall. He opened the double doors at the end, and ushered me into a luxurious living-room, with plate-glass windows and French doors on to an expansive sandstone terrace with a stunning view of Sydney Harbour. This is how the rich in Sydney lived.

As I gazed out, a figure moved towards me and I readjusted my focus back to the room.

There was no mistaking Lady Ophelia, but the media photos didn't do her justice. She was forty-five, but didn't look it: the fine English skin, spared from the blazing sun that Aussie women grow up with. Possibly helped by not having to work for a living, with its parasitic stresses. And no doubt ably assisted by expensive French skin products.

Or so I read. All I ever use is a daub of Vaseline. Well, it's on the supermarket shelf, right along from the condoms and lube. Need I say more?

Back to the babe at hand. Lady Ophelia sashayed over to me and shook my hand, firmly yet femininely. She was tall, with sapphire-blue eyes and sumptuous blonde hair. She wore little make-up, but it was classy. Whilst slim, she was well bosomed, and I could tell they were natural. Her salmon-pink silk blouse was taut enough to whisper, 'I've got magnificent breasts, so admire', but not so tight as to scream, 'I'm a tart, so come play'. Simply put, Lady Ophelia was smoking hot and I was barring up already.

'Lady Ophelia, it's a pleasure to meet you.'

'Mr Kenmare, welcome. I see you've done your research.'

'It goes with the territory.'

She looked me in the eye, longer than the situation needed, and then longer than decorum permitted. There was a smouldering desire in those beautiful blues. My erection completed itself.

'My husband will be through shortly. Come and sit down. And please, Ophelia is fine.' She smiled as I sat, trying to angle myself to conceal my boner.

'Thank you. I'm Harry.'

'Yes, I know.' She looked at me again for an indecently long instant.

At that moment, a side door opened and two teenage girls came in giggling, a large dog in their wake. They were cut from the same fine cloth as their mother. They were simply stunning. Eighteen and nineteen, I'd read. I figured they'd break a lot of hearts along the way, if they weren't already.

Everything in this place so far was expensive and beautiful, and got my juices flowing. Fuck, even the Labrador was hot, if you're into that sort of thing, that is.

A sudden noise and another door opened abruptly. Marcus Standing marched into the room, a young man at his side. I stood up.

Standing didn't bother with my outstretched hand and the look on his face likened me to a shit stain on his carpet.

'Mr Kenmare, I'll get straight to the point and then Lionel here will discuss the details. I've got better things to be doing.'

What a wanker.

'Certainly, Mr Standing.'

'My niece, Tracey, is missing. A journalist is sniffing around. Suggested Tracey is on the streets selling herself to feed her drug habit.'

'An all too frequent and sad combination.'

He held up his hand and sneered. 'Don't interrupt me, Kenmare. I can't afford to have Tracey found by the media. A lot of people would like to do me harm.'

No shit Sherlock. But I said nothing.

'Find her so we can get her into a clinic. Understood?'

'Crystal clear. That's what I'm good at.'

'So I understand. But that's as much as I care to know about your grubby world, Kenmare. I don't like your type, or your part of society. You'll deal with Lionel from now on.'

Before he could turn away, my Irish genes rebelled.

'I'm sure our feelings are mutual, Mr Standing. The fact I'm here to find your niece who's a druggie prostitute selling her minge in the gutter would seem to indicate the line between your lofty universe and my grubby world is not that well drawn.' I smiled at him as insolently as I could.

If glares could kill, I would have been an instant corpse.

There was complete and utter silence in the room. These four walls were clearly not used to anyone answering back, especially a grubby working man. Standing turned on his heel and stormed out of the room, slamming the door.

The snivelling Lionel, struggling to regain his composure after witnessing his master being reproved, invited me to a table.

As I sat down, I looked over at Lady Ophelia. She was staring at me, trying to maintain an altogether different composure: I could see her nipples were hard. She beamed lustfully and walked out the opposite way to her husband. The girls and the dog followed.

So, according to my briefing, Tracey had moved in two years ago after her parents died. She was sixteen then. Despite everything being provided for her, she fell in with a bad crowd, and started on drugs.

Provided with everything except a loving family, I guessed, but said nothing. I left the house with a much fatter wallet and a reinforced contempt for the rich and powerful.

As I drove down the driveway, in my mirror I saw Lady Ophelia watching me from a window. There was no mistaking the smile on her lovely face. I wouldn't have said 'no' to putting an even bigger one on it.

– **3** –

So, here I was, Tracey (or Smokey) sitting in my car stroking my obelisk-like cock, and me as horny as a goat on Viagra. As I said, what's a man to do?

Maybe you're thinking my strong, righteous sense of professional ethics prevailed. No, it was the track marks on her arms and the ulcers in her mouth that won out. My cock wasn't going anywhere near Tracey's orifices. No amount of rubber coating would have persuaded me otherwise. When I pulled two hundred out of my wallet, she moved to unzip my trousers. I stayed her hand, gave her the four fifties, and let her down gently.

'Babe, there's a reason a private detective has picked you up.'

'Because he wants a fuck.'

Crying shame she wasn't clean and chatting to me in a bar, because some private dick is what she would have got.

'No, I've been paid to find you.'

She sat back, withdrawing her hand from my bulging crotch.

'What?'

I didn't want her running. I don't like running. Plus when a bloke like me is chasing a tart in a short skirt down the street, people tend to call the cops. Or at least you'd hope they would.

I went for the safe option. I pulled out another hundred, slid it into her boob tube, and let my hand linger on her breast. Well, she did have great tits and I was paying.

'If you listen to what I've got to say, then there'll be even more. The cash, I mean.'

Her eyes perked up enough to show I'd hit the right button. I kept my wallet within view to ensure her undivided attention.

'Your stinking-rich uncle wants you off the street and into rehab. The story I got was that he doesn't need the media publicity of a niece in his care doing the gear and walking the street. Bad for business apparently.'

Her snort of derision threatened to bring up the last load of swallowed semen.

'In his care, my fucking arse!' She spat the words out. 'Did you believe the cunt?'

'Well,' I said, 'whilst I would agree with your last description of him, I didn't have any reason to doubt the story.'

'Not too smart for a detective.'

I gave her a dumb look with a matching inane grin. If I gave her the feeling of the upper hand for a minute, she'd talk to me.

'I'm listening, babe.'

'Mr Respectable used to fuck me every weekend. Started a month after I moved in. That's why I ran away. The gear makes the pain less. Get me?'

She was looking me square in the face, her eyes a mixture of anger at her life and desperation for being believed.

'I'm sorry, Tracey.' I touched her face gently. Tears rolled languorously out of both eyes.

'Thanks.'

I knew the answer, but the question had to be asked.

'Thought about reporting it?'

She snorted. 'Nobody's going to believe me, especially against him.'

It was getting dark outside now and a breeze had picked up. A sudden gust sent a rain of purple jacaranda flowers down onto the car. What the fuck was I going to do with this girl?

'I'd like to help you.'

'Okay, go back to the fucker and tell him to pay me my money.'

'What? You asking for cash to keep you quiet?'

'Better than that. I got a film.'

Now that got my interest.

'Last time he did me I set my phone on video. Now I've told him it's a million bucks for the film or else.'

I could sympathize with her, but I knew damned well Standing would never pay. Not only because his type couldn't stand to lose. From a purely practical point of view, he would never be sure she hadn't made copies.

'Here, watch.'

She pulled out her phone.

I watched her fellating a man, only visible from chest down. Then he pulled his cock out and pushed her back onto a bed.

'Doggy-style, bitch!' was clearly audible. Maybe Standing's voice, but I wouldn't chance it with a jury.

Tracey got on all fours. The man climbed onto the bed and started fucking her. The face was definitely him. Okay, I'd give that a run in court.

He grunted as he came. He pulled out, slapped her on the bum and said, 'Now thank sugar Daddy for everything he gives you.' No mistaking Standing's commanding tone this time.

'Thank you, Daddy.'

Tracey turned it off.

'See, I got the fucker on toast.'

She seemed convinced her plan was foolproof. I wished it was, but it wasn't.

'Sure have,' I said anyway.

It wasn't, because whilst the sex was unarguable, consent wasn't.

If I were in Standing's place, then I'd say, 'Sure, I'm a red-blooded man who gave in to a little temptress. You might think I'm weak, immoral even, but I'm not a criminal. She asked for it and I gave it to her.'

Plenty of guys have beaten a rap with that defence: sometimes truthful, sometimes not. But that's how the system works. A prosecutor would depend on Tracey's evidence convincing a jury she was actually a victim. And Standing would have the best lawyers out there. I didn't like Tracey's chances. The trial would be like getting raped all over again.

I lit a smoke and gave her one. I looked at the collection of beautiful purple flowers now adorning my windscreen.

A much darker thought jumped up and smacked me between the eyes. If Tracey couldn't ever give evidence, then there wouldn't even be a case.

Fuck! Standing didn't want her in rehab, he wanted her in the fucking morgue. That's why he needed to find her.

I looked at her. I thought of Hobbes and life being nasty, brutish, and short. I suspected Tracey's was getting shorter rapidly.

'I'm not going to tell him where you are.'

'Okay. Get me my million and I'll cut you in.'

I gave her another cigarette to smoke as I copied her video onto my laptop. That done, I put the computer back under the seat and returned her phone.

'So, when are you going to talk to the arsehole?' she asked.

'In the morning. How about we meet back here same time tomorrow?'

'Cool.' She looked steamily at me. 'Sure you don't want to fuck me?'

'Tracey, you're a babe, but this is strictly work.'

'That's too bad. I reckon I would've actually enjoyed your cock.'

She rubbed my crotch farewell, pouted, and got out of the car.

'See you, handsome.'

And with that she was gone, back onto the pavement.

I started the car and pulled away. As I got to the traffic lights, I looked in my mirror. A large, black BMW had pulled up. She was striking a pose next to it. As the lights went green, and I turned onto Wattle Street, she was leaning on the sill of the passenger door.

Smokey was straight on to the next client.

– 4 –

It was pissing down the next morning. I stared at the deluge through my dirty office window, drinking a coffee and alternating between confusion and dread.

I'd rung the Standing house at 9.30 a.m. and spoken to the slimy Lionel, explaining I'd located Tracey. I repeated her demand and mentioned the video. Lionel seemed to take it all in his stride, as if I'd been talking about the weather or the traffic. He simply said my assignment was complete, the outstanding payment was in my account, and he hung up.

Now I was perplexed, but also worried.

I rang Tracey's mobile. No answer. Maybe nothing in that, junkies don't tend to surface before lunchtime.

I switched on the radio for some music to distract my unpleasant thoughts and continued gazing out at the wet, grimy city. The news bulletin came on. I froze at the first story.

> Police have identified the young woman whose body was found under the Wentworth Park viaduct yesterday evening. She was eighteen-year-old Tracey Standing, niece of Sydney billionaire, Marcus Standing. Ms Standing had been living with her uncle's family since the tragic death of her parents two years ago. It is understood she had been suffering from severe depression. The local Police Commander said that there were no suspicious circumstances and it appeared Ms Standing had taken her own life. A brief will be prepared for the Coroner. The Standing family lawyer has asked for their privacy to be respected at this sad time. If you, or someone you know, needs support, call Lifeline on 13 11 14.

'Fuck!' I screamed at the window. Had Standing got to her already? Or was it an awful coincidence?

But in my business I don't believe in coincidences.

I got on the phone to an old mate, still operational in the police. Detective Sergeant Brian Durham was cagey when I mentioned Tracey, but he agreed to meet me on the q.t. in the Chinese Gardens.

An hour later, Brian and I parted ways. I'd told him about my case. His last words to me were haunting.

'Tread carefully, Harry. These people run the whole system, and they are fucking ruthless. My advice, mate, is to drop it. Life's never been fair anyway, and you can't bring Tracey back. She probably would have died somehow soon enough anyway'.

His cynicism was well founded, but painful nonetheless.

He'd shown me some CCTV footage from an office foyer in the street where I'd met Tracey. I saw her and that black BMW, as I had when I left her. Then I saw what came after my turning the corner yesterday: Standing's ex-military thug hurling Tracey into the back seat. That bastard must have followed me.

I suggested to Brian she'd been killed with a hotshot. He agreed, but told me the case had been closed down from the very top. It was officially a suicide.

– 5 –

I was back at my desk, as mad as hell at the world. I hated the arrogant wankers of the Establishment at the best of times, but I was particularly loathful today.

I rang the Standing house and asked for Lady Ophelia.

'Hello?' The steamy voice.

'Ophelia, it's Harry Kenmare.'

'Harry, I'm glad you called.'

'You know he was raping her, don't you?'

There was a slight pause before she replied. Steamy became sad. 'I knew things were going on.'

'Why didn't you do something?'

'Tracey wouldn't confide in me. The best I could do was to tell Marcus that if he ever touched my daughters, then I would destroy him.'

My turn to pause.

'Ophelia, why stay with him? You could take your pick of all sorts of decent guys.'

'I'm not proud of this, Harry. Marcus needs me for the aristocratic connections. Being my husband opens doors in London. And I need his money for the lifestyle for my daughters and I.'

'But doesn't your own family have money? As you said, you are aristocracy.'

'In title, absolutely. But with empty coffers. My father blew the family fortune: numerous mistresses and an addiction to Monte Carlo. Without Marcus, I'd be destitute. As I said, I'm not proud of myself, but we all make our choices in life.'

'So, it's purely a marriage of convenience then?'

'If that's your way of asking if we sleep together, Harry, then the answer is I've only slept with him twice, ever. Hence my two daughters.'

'Oh, I see.'

'And please, go back to the Australian directness. I prefer it, and it suits you much better.'

I smiled, despite my mood. A plan was forming in my twisted mind. And she wanted directness.

'Okay, Ophelia, how about you come over to my place and let me ravish you senseless?'

'You see? Much more your style. It just rolled off your tongue. I'll see you in two hours.'

I gave her my address and hung up. There was going to be a lot more rolling off my tongue shortly.

One more call had to be made first.

I convinced Lionel if he didn't put me through to his boss, I was going to find him and break his legs.

'What do you want, Kenmare? I've paid your bill and then some.' Arrogance and disdain oozed down the phone line.

'Standing, I know you raped Tracey. I know you had your henchman kill her. And I've got a copy of the video she took.'

He guffawed as only the arrogantly contemptuous can.

'Kenmare, you grub, you can't touch me. I don't care if you've got a copy of the video. You're an ex-cop. You know that without her there'd never be a trial. It's just a sex tape, all consensual of course. Besides, I know all the right people. There won't even be any questions asked.'

I clenched my teeth as I listened to the cold, hard truth.

'You'll keep, Standing.'

That fucking laugh again.

'Kenmare, go suck shit. That's what you're good at. You're nothing in the scheme of things. Piss off back to the gutter you crawled out of.'

The phone went dead.

I wasn't finished with this cunt yet.

– 6 –

Lady Ophelia came through the door of my apartment looking like Helen entering the gates of Troy. She was smoking hot. And hot to trot as it turned out.

'Drink?' I offered.

'Bedroom, now!'

Who was I to argue?

She stripped faster than a late guest at a Roman orgy.

The next two hours rivalled the most memorable of my life. We did it all, every way imaginable. Lady O enjoyed six orgasms, I stunned myself with four: a Kenmare record.

When we were utterly exhausted, we lay back on the bed and finally drank the Sancerre I had on ice.

She told me it had been the most incredible sexual experience of her life. I believed her. I told her it was right up there for me, too. I didn't go into detail, mind you. She didn't need to hear my dissolute biography.

As she got dressed to leave, she said something almost prescient.

'Harry, I so wish that creep of a husband of mine could have seen us doing all that.'

'Really?'

'It would consume him inside. Seeing me being taken by another man. He hates losing. I am going to tell him, and that I did it to avenge Tracey. It will cut him like a knife.'

I looked at her, trying not to smile. 'I'm a firm believer in karma. Standing will get what he deserves eventually.'

'Possibly. Meantime, I just want to look after my girls.'

'Understood.'

She kissed me, stroking my cheek, grabbed her handbag, and left the apartment. And my life: I never saw her again.

I reached behind the headboard of the bed and retrieved the recording unit. I'm sure the micro lens posing as a thumbtack on the wall poster winked at me. I poured myself a large Jameson.

The footage was, even if I say so myself, worthy of a few gongs at the porn film awards.

I duplicated the file, editing it for the highlights.

I attached the short, medley version to an email.

I picked up my phone, again mentioned violence to Lionel, and then I was speaking to Standing.

'Kenmare, I told you to disappear, you grotty, little man. What don't you understand about that?'

'Open your email, Standing. Interesting video for you, and it's not Tracey.'

There was silence on the other end, but I could hear keystrokes.

'Watch the video clip, cunty.'

A minute went by: enough for him to hear his wife proclaiming her backdoor virginity and to watch me deflowering her arse. A pack of wolves couldn't have howled more convincingly than she did.

Standing exploded.

'You fucking piece of shit! I'll destroy you, Kenmare!'

I was ready for the 'I'm all powerful' onslaught.

'Whatever, Standing. Aside from the video of you raping Tracey, and aside from this sensational footage of your wife impaled on my cock — and she loved it, by the way — there's another compelling reason you'll never come near me.'

'Oh, really? What's that you piece of garbage?'

'If I ever detect the slightest whiff of you anywhere near me, the next video will be me chock-a-block up your two daughters. And I bet they're anal virgins, like your wife used to be. Goodbye, fuckstain.'

I put the phone down, smiled, and poured myself another drink.

* * *

– Case #2 –

WHITE POWDER, BLACK LEATHER, GREY BADGES

... she sashayed over. No amount of rum would ever call her pretty. What she oozed was sex, lashings of it.

- Ken Bruen

WHITE POWDER, BLACK LEATHER, GREY BADGES

– 1 –

Naked, aching, lying on cold, wet tiles in an outlaw bikie gang's clubhouse. Hot, acrid urine streaming over my face, head, chest. Was that asparagus? Not a usual bikie type of food. And how much could one human bladder hold? I'd seen elephants at the zoo finish more quickly. How much more? That's what I was asking myself.

You're possibly asking yourself where the hell was he and what happened to him? Sounds as if he crossed the wrong black-leather-clad association of upstanding citizens, got done over, and was now playing a human urinal for their sport.

And my butt-naked, throbbingly sore, and toilet-wet circumstances with the Satan's Hogs Motorcycle Club arose from them being my clients. Yep, me being PI Harry Kenmare, I'd take on pretty well any client (paedophiles and rapists need not apply) as long as they were paying well. Shit, I'd even take on a case for a politician or a banker, at an inflated rate of course. So, the boss man of the Sydney chapter of the Satan's Hogs, Archie Longman, was welcome by comparison.

But right now it was all piss and pain.

– 2 –

Archie Longman and I went way back: back to when I was a detective on the Force, in the Holdup Squad, and he was an armed robber. Naturally our paths crossed. He ended up doing some serious prison time. I ended up doing some different hard time: my little girl, Orla, was raped and murdered by paedophiles.

Oh, yeah, and the green-bottle problems. You get that.

Yeah, okay, so I bashed a prisoner. Moral majority types, cue for disapproving tutting, and then piss off. Said prisoner was a child molester, and I'd just lost my kid to his kind. Yep, breaking his jaw felt good, badge or not.

I 'got out' of the Force, and Longman eventually got out of jail. I became a PI, and Longman became a bikie drug-dealer. We met again when he needed my skills to track down his niece's rapists, recently paroled. I did the job and delivered. Gave him an address. The rapists died, of course: executed. Good riddance in my books. Anyway, Longman and I kept in touch. Then two weeks ago, he gave me a call.

– 3 –

A month earlier, a Hogs' shipment had been too easily intercepted by the Drug Squad, not normally known for their effectiveness, at least not when it came to upholding the law. Turned out one of the Hogs' recent recruits was an informer. Well, he only got to do one job for the cops: Longman and his sergeant-at-arms, Rocco 'The Ratfucker' Corsi, dealt with the matter promptly. Corsi didn't get his moniker from having a sexual predilection for small furry rodents. Well, apart from enjoying more beaver than a Canadian lake. No, he was the exterminator for the rats in the ranks: a vital function in organized crime. Anyway, Longman and The Ratfucker had got the truth out of the snitch courtesy of a blowtorch to his testicles. Then they cut them off and fed them to him, along with his cock. It was Corsi's trademark technique, and the whole underworld knew it.

Soon word came down the street the same shipment was up for sale, courtesy of one Detective Sergeant Jonny 'The Shagger' Chilvers.

Now there was an arsehole I knew from my days in the detectives. He was an ex-copper from the Metropolitan Police in London. Fancied more sunshine in his life, like quite a few British coppers. Except the others weren't as bent as Jonny. Anyway, Chilvers had licked the arse of some very senior NSW officer at an international event, and so his salivating sycophancy, along with all his bad habits, emigrated down under. And The Shagger got himself a job with the police in Sydney.

I remembered him well. His nickname, which he had given himself, like only a true wanker does, was his trademark. He was infamous for committing the one cardinal sin in the detective brotherhood: fucking the women of other detectives. Pretty well every sort of immoral or illegal misbehaviour went down okay in those days, but not fucking another demon's missus. Wife, girlfriend, or even dirty bird on the side, of which there were many around the squads, the Code stated you didn't touch. Simply not on, not bloody cool. Never, ever.

So, the phone call from Longman.

'Kenmare, you know these cunts. I want you to do the job and get the goods on this arsewipe, Chilvers. Then we'll turn him over to the Integrity Commission. He can look forward to some very hard time inside. We could take him out, but that'd bring down way too much heat. Plus I want to send a message to the other bent pigs. There's a healthy pay-day in it for you.'

'I get that, Longman, but going up against the cops is a hard gig. Chilvers is as corrupt as sin, but he's still got a badge and some mates in the Squad, most of whom are bent as well.'

'Listen Kenmare, you and me are mates of sorts, and I trust you. Coming from me, that's saying a lot for an ex-cop. Now you want this gig or not? It's twenty grand cash.'

Yeah, the magic number sorted out all of my qualms in an instant.

I like to live as hard as possible, none of which is cheap in Sydney. Especially my tastes at three magnificent local bordellos. The women are stellar, but they know how to fleece you. Well, hardly surprising, that is their line of work. And I love them for it.

'I'm in, Longman.'

'Cool.'

He explained what was going down.

A local Lebanese drug baron, Aziz el-Masri, was arranging to buy the shipment off Chilvers. One of el-Masri's gang was double-dealing and had informed to Corsi, for a price. Not much honour in those esteemed ranks.

So, Longman wanted me to do some top quality surveillance of the deal meeting: get Chilvers recorded for posterity taking a $250k bundle of cash for the 5kg of coke. Sounded simple enough, for a PI like me. As long as I didn't get caught. Chilvers would shoot me as soon as look at me if he thought he was going down. And he'd dress it up so it looked as if I were in with the dealers instead. It'd be a fair kill in the eyes of the city's finest, and they'd drink to a job well done. This was a tough gig. And my sometime offsider, Trev, who specialized in surveillance, was doing an assignment down in Melbourne. So, it was down to me, solo: an even tougher gig. No room for fuck-ups.

– 4 –

Late afternoon was the time. A lonely car park in the Ku-ring-gai Chase National Park north of Sydney was the place. I'd got there two hours early, parking my hired van in a different car park and covering the intervening two kilometres on foot.

I've never bothered with buying any wheels myself, despite our car-obsessed culture. When you drink as regularly, and as heartily, as I do, you depend on the taxi service. Or Trev, when he's around.

I walked along a bush track, with a rucksack, looking pretty much like the average bushwalker out for an afternoon stroll through nature. Except for what was in my pack, that is. First up, a digital Pentax SLR with a wide-aperture, big zoom lens. And I mean 'big' of the 'fuck off big' variety: a new piece of kit I'd bought for the occasion. The camera's companion in the backpack also screamed out 'fuck off': a shortened Remington 12-gauge pump-action shotgun, always one of my favourite weapons from my days on the Force. Except the official police ones weren't cut-down. And strapped to my belt was my trusty Smith & Wesson .38 Special revolver. Yeah, okay, a bit old school, but I'd never lost the comfortable feel of it, and I was Speedy Gonzales when it came to ditching the six spent shells and reloading. I had three speed-loaders nestled on the opposite side of my waist. I was certainly prepared, just in case things went to shit. But I reminded myself that on this beautiful afternoon my role was only as a hidden observer in the bushes: a voyeur of vengeance, so to speak.

I cut off the track as it ran about a hundred metres behind the target car park and worked my way up onto a slight rise, dense with wattle bushes in full September bloom: our beautiful national flower. A sharp contrast to the corruption to come below: our ugly national sport. I positioned myself behind some boulders with a clear view of the gravel parking lot, and settled in to wait. The pervasive scent of the golden wattles was idyllic. I threw a short lens on the Pentax and grabbed a few shots of botanical beauty, satisfy my sensitive side, you understand. Then I switched lenses, back to the zoom monster.

I lay back against a rock to wait out the next hour and a half.

Ten minutes later, I heard a car engine. Far too early for the drug deal. I sat up and saw a late model Audi pull in. There were two young people in it, a boy no more than nineteen driving, and a similarly aged girl in the passenger seat. Must have borrowed mummy's or daddy's car. Or perhaps they simply came from one of those North Shore suburbs where the kids are given a luxury German motor as a present for passing their driving test. They had music on, some of the non-melodic shit all the young ones listened to. I could hear her laughing.

They got out of the car, and I could see them better. He was your typical stringy, pimply young kid. She was seriously fucking hot: short skirt and a boob tube, showing a sensational midriff. And she had a rack on her that would have made the Pope tumescent. Me, I was enjoying the view, and considering getting seriously tumescent myself. This young lad was punching well above his weight. He got a packet out of his jeans pocket. She started rubbing his chest and kissing him. I was close enough to hear them, given the serene surrounds. And that was in spite of the doof doof beat.

'I got this for us,' he teased, smiling at her and waving a sachet of white powder in front of her.

'Cool! Let's blow and then fuck,' she replied.

Sweet. Unexpected entertainment before my main event, and they'd be long gone before the real shit arrived.

Pimples poured the powder into a little mound on the bonnet of the Audi. He passed her a crisp $100 note as he used a credit card to line up the coke. By the time he was done, she'd rolled the note like an expert (obviously no virgin in this regard, or any other I guessed) and they took turns to snort away. The white snow was gone in a minute: clearly not amateurs.

I smiled. Seeing the young, rich ones getting into the upper-class lifestyle so easily merely cemented my view of the Establishment. Their respectable parents were no doubt big-end-of-town lawyers and bankers, political players and influencers, telling all of us plebs how to lead our lives in a proper manner.

Ah yes, the scent of smouldering hypocrites is never far from the nostrils in this fucked-up city.

'Let's do it now,' the girl said, stroking the lad's crotch.

'You sure, Ali? What if someone comes by?'

'Nathan, fuck me now or I'll put what a loser you are on Facebook.'

Yep, if you don't do her right here and now, mate, you are a complete bloody loser. Plus, I'll come down there and do her for you. That thought did have me barring up.

'Okay, in the back seat?' the timid Nathan asked.

'No,' she said, dropping her skirt and peeling off a G string.

Oh, fuck me, she had a total Brazilian as well. As she parked her sweet, little arse on the car bonnet, she pulled off her top. Yep, they were puppies to die for. So, what was a man to do? Pick up the Pentax, of course!

As Nathan clumsily dropped his strides and briefs, I took some classic images of Ali spreadeagled on the Audi's shining metalwork. In my viewfinder I could see her pussy glistening with wet, adolescent desire.

Nathan was clearly a greenhorn. He went straight in for the main act. I was busy photographing the whole shebang. Now, if I hadn't needed to stay covert, with bigger fish to fry, I might have gone on down there and given him some manly advice. Fuck, might even have demonstrated, if she were up for it. Might? Who am I trying to kid? It would have been game on. Yes, PI Harry Kenmare would have eaten her pussy until Ali screamed for mercy. Then, and only then, would my cock have impaled her. I would've shown her what a real man was for.

Brings to mind a line from one of my favourite crime authors, Christa Faust: that a man who can't eat pussy is a waste of space, or something similar. Bang on, I reckon.

Nathan, however, was done in less than two minutes. Poor prick. He had a lot to learn. Well, at least he'd got it inside her, and not blown his load beforehand.

Ali put her clothes back on, and he pulled up his trousers.

To see all that wasted opportunity, all Ali's gorgeous flesh so under enjoyed, was enough to make a real man cry.

The Audi left the car park. I perused all the images on my Pentax screen. I peered long and hard at Ali's wet pussy. Oh boy, what I would do with that. Still, back to work, damn it.

–5–

It was an hour later when I heard the next vehicle engine, but it stopped well short of the entrance to the car park. It sounded like a V8, and hunting through my viewfinder, I saw what looked like a Ford F250 pick-up parked off the road about seventy metres away. I couldn't see any heads. Maybe this was backup for the Lebs.

Then I heard another engine. A Commodore, obviously an unmarked police car, roared into the car park and slid to a halt on the gravel. Chilvers was in the driver's seat.

Wanker behind the wheel, wanker of a man, I always say.

My blood boiled when I saw the cunt's face. It'd been a long time. But I didn't forget, let alone forgive. And the smug, arrogant smirk that always adorned his pasty face: that superior, contemptuous look certain Englishmen pour on the inferior colonials down under. Fuck, I wanted to wipe it off. But damn it, today was surveillance only.

Chilvers stayed in his car, until another vehicle screamed into the lot: a Subaru WRX with all the rev-head trimmings (the Lebanese chariot of choice). More wankers. So, it was on, it seemed.

There were three guys in the Subaru, and they got out as soon as the beast was stationary. One of them had a briefcase. The other two made no effort to downplay their AK-47s.

Chilvers got out of his car, looking as smug as ever, carrying a sports bag. He walked to the middle of the space between the two vehicles. The Leb with the briefcase fronted him.

'Got the gear, *detective*?' The Leb stressed the last word, making a point.

'Yeah,' replied Chilvers. 'But I want to see the cash.'

The man flicked opened the case, holding it up. I could see the bundles of used notes, all fifties. Click, click, click went the Pentax.

'Let's see the gear, *detective*.' He stressed the word again. 'And we want to test it first.'

'Here you go.' Chilvers opened his bag and pulled out a plastic bundle. I glimpsed a collection of them piled inside the bag. More photos.

The Leb took the packet and went back to his mates. They cut it open, produced a testing bag, and swilled the sample in the liquid. The testing guy nodded at the main man, who went back to Chilvers.

'All good, *detective*. Now we'll weigh it.'

They all went over to the boot of the WRX and the testing dude brought out some scales. Once satisfied, the main man turned to Chilvers.

'We gotta deal, *detective*. Here you go.'

I was wondering if there was some double-cross coming, but not even the Lebs would risk hell on earth by gunning down a demon, as corrupt as he was. The ensuing wrath of the squads would be far too damaging for business.

Chilvers took the briefcase of cash, an even smugger grin smeared across his face, and left the drugs with the Lebs.

I had it all, and I mean all, recorded for posterity. Oh, and for the Integrity Commission, via Longman.

Job done.

Or so I thought.

Before Chilvers could get back into his police car, all hell broke loose.

Three black-leather dudes erupted from the bush on the far side of the car park, two with shotguns and one with an M16. A couple of shotgun blasts pummelled the Subaru.

The Lebs took cover and returned fire with the AK-47s. The bikies certainly weren't Longman's gang. Their proudly worn colours were different. One of them took an AK bullet and fell, wounded, but still reloading his shotgun.

Chilvers, meanwhile, had his Glock 9mm out and was screaming 'Police!' at them. He came out from behind the fender of the Commodore and let a couple of rounds go. To no avail. Yeah, I always said he was a fucking lightweight. The bikie with the M16, however, was not. He let a well-aimed burst go and Chilvers went down, looking as if he'd taken at least three hits.

More shotgun blasts, car windows imploding, metal panels getting drilled, hails of bullets from the two AKs, and the M16. A total cacophony of cordite and hot lead.

I couldn't see how this was going to pan out.

Then one of the Lebs took an M16 round straight through his head. One fewer. Okay, maybe the tide was turning. One of his compatriots screamed something in Arabic. He stood up and emptied his AK clip. He hit two of the bikies, including the already wounded one. He now looked critical.

Time for me to mix it up a bit. Never was much good as a mere observer. But I wanted them gone, needed them gone, because I desperately wanted to walk over to Chilvers and smile at him, before he died.

I shouted, 'Police! Don't move!' I accompanied my yell with letting two rounds go from my .38. Not that I could have hit a barn door from this distance, but hitting anything wasn't the objective. Then I lowered my voice to become my invisible offsider, and called, 'Police!', as I cranked the pump-action. That noise, unmistakeable to those in the know, got their attention. I gave three blasts, managing to spray one of the remaining Lebs with some pellets in his arse.

Some more shouted Arabic, and the two surviving Lebs were into their Subaru, now riddled with enough ammunition holes to resemble a Baghdad taxi.

As the Subaru roared out of the car park, one Leb gave a parting burst of ineffective fire at the bikies. I let more rounds go from both my weapons just for good measure.

The two still-standing bikies, one limping badly, headed for the bushes. One stopped to confirm their mate was dead, and then scurried off. I heard their F250 come to life, and they were off.

I waited until the sound of both engines had disappeared altogether. I reloaded my .38, and walked the short distance into the car park. None of the three bodies on the ground was moving at all. With my trusty gat ready in front of me, I walked over to the Leb. Two wide-open eyes stared fixedly at the sky, a red, dribbling hole almost perfectly centred between them. Yep, he was on his way to claim his seventy-three virgins, or whatever shit these people believed.

The bikie was slumped against a log railing at the edge of the lot about ten metres away. He, too, was gazing lifelessly in front of him. I could see at least four abdominal wounds, and blood was dripping off his chin, remnants of the stream that had spewed out from his lungs before his breathing stopped.

I turned back around, spotting the open sports bag full of packets of white powder. The Lebs' scales lay broken on the gravel. I looked further, over to Chilvers. No movement, but there was the closed briefcase I'd seen the cash in.

Bugger me. Not only did I have the photos for my assignment, now largely redundant of course, but I had Longman's stolen drug shipment, and I had the dealers' buy money for it. My lucky day. I'd sure need to grab a lottery ticket on the way home tonight.

I hoped to hell Chilvers was still alive, even if only barely. But enough to recognize me and watch my smirking face.

As I got to him, I could hear faint gurgling. He had four bullet hits, but the real problem one for him was the lung shot: he was slowly drowning in his own blood. Couldn't happen to a nicer bloke, if you asked me.

But then I'm not exactly known for showing any compassion to cunts.

His eyes were shut, so I gave him a kick in the ribs. His eyes eased open. There was a flicker of recognition, tinged with fear. Good.

'Hello, cunty. How are you these days?' I sniggered. 'Purely rhetorical. Not too fucking flash by the looks of it. Well, they do say corruption doesn't pay, Chilvers.'

'Hel … Help … Help me …' wheezed out through the blood clogging his mouth.

I laughed again, a real gut-wrencher this time. I pulled on some latex gloves. I crouched next to him, momentarily savouring the faint gleam of hope in his eyes. I undid his belt and yanked his trousers and shorts down to his knees. That glimmer of hope extinguished in a millisecond.

I pulled a Commando dagger out of the sheath strapped to my ankle.

Always carry a backup weapon, because you never know.

'Yeah, I'll help you, Chilvers. To die like the mongrel dog you are.'

It was a great pity he couldn't talk more: I would've enjoyed hearing him plead for his life.

Now, maybe you're thinking I was going to finish him off for being such a grossly corrupt cop. Understandable, even justifiable, to my mind anyway. But no, I'd happily have left him there to bleed to death for that sin. No, this was personal. The messiest encounters always are.

Remember what I said about Chilvers breaking the Code and fucking other detectives' women? Well, one of them was my ex-wife. We'd actually already split, and I didn't particularly care for her, but the Code was still the Code. We pretty well all respected it.

But not Chilvers. I'd heard he even bragged about it in the bar, and that was intolerable. Capital, in fact. I thought about Nietzsche, fighting monsters, staring into the abyss until it stared back into you.

Yeah, I like Nietzsche, but the abyss stared back into me a long time ago. I live in the fucking abyss.

I grabbed The Shagger's penis and scrotum in my left hand.

'Remember fucking my ex-missus, Chilvers? And all those other blokes' women?'

He stared at me, enough vim left in his eyes to show pure terror.

'Well, this is for all of them, and for the Code. Which you never took any notice of. But never too late to learn.'

I rammed the blade into his perineum and hacked in a circular motion. I lifted his junk clear as blood ran onto the ground, swirling in the sandy coloured gravel.

'Open wide, cunt. It's the last headjob you'll ever have!'

I pulled his jaw down with my knife hand, and rammed his bloodied tackle into his mouth.

I smiled at him, as I had fantasized about doing, whilst he gagged to death on his own genitals.

I carved an 'R' into his forehead. That was The Ratfucker's signature he always left, aside from the genital surgery. This crime scene would look like exactly what it was: a falling out between assorted drug-dealers. Bikies, Lebs, and a crooked detective, what a grand collective.

Only PI Harry Kenmare would be left off the list of credits. And that suited me perfectly.

As I collected the various bags of goodies and the assorted weaponry, a couple of kookaburras let rip with their cackling chorus up in a gum tree. Maybe they were enjoying the irony.

– 6 –

Two hours later, I pulled into the compound at the Satan's Hogs' clubhouse. As I unloaded the drugs, the cash, and the guns onto Longman's coffee table, he and The Ratfucker looked on in awe.

'What the fuck, Kenmare?'

'It's a bit of an involved story, Longman.'

Rocco produced some beers. We cracked the cans and I gave them the low-down.

Longman counted $100k out of the briefcase and slid the delicious-looking stack across the table to me.

'Your share, mate. I'm assuming you don't want any of the snow?'

'No. Thanks anyway. Frankly I think it should all be legalized. Would stop all sorts of shit going down.'

Longman cackled hard.

'Mate, no one would make any real money out of it then. And half the big end of town actually controls this trade. People like us are really only the middle level, despite appearances.'

I nodded in grudging acknowledgement of the unsavoury truth as I downed my beer.

'Mate, I'll take the Glock though, if that's okay?'

'Of course.' He slid the police-issue gun across the table.

'Angie!' he yelled.

A moment later, this fine-looking and deliciously slutty bikie moll walked into the room.

I looked at her. She would be one disgustingly sordid fuck. And disgracefully memorable.

'A bonus, Kenmare,' grinned Longman.

I was confused.

'Angie, take Mr Kenmare here off to your room for some real appreciation from us. A real Satan's Hogs extravaganza of the flesh.'

'No worries, Arch.'

She looked over at me with a wicked smile on her face. Skank itself couldn't have looked skankier.

'This way, honey.'

So, now I was lying in an en suite bathroom to the living quarters of Angie, who was covered in tatts, and I mean smothered in them, including the python that coiled around both her nipple-ringed breasts, went over her left shoulder, down her spine, into her butt crack, and literally up her arsehole. Angie with large, firm tits, a magnificent arse, and a complete inability to even spell morals.

For the last two hours, Angie had been fucking sensational with all three of her orifices. Well, she would be: most bikie tarts get their sex-ed classes with all three holes filled simultaneously. It had been a wonderful surprise to find how splendidly tight her anus still was, considering it had probably seen more traffic than an L.A. freeway.

And that full bladder, by the way, was hers.

She had insisted on having a final orgasm by masturbating herself as I took my first ever golden shower. It was clearly a huge turn-on for her, since she came, screaming, as the last dribble of piss spattered on my face.

'Had enough, Harry?' she grinned at me.

'Angie, babe, you are fucking incredible.'

'I know.' She squatted over my face, wiping her moist pussy all over me. 'Just leaving my mark, big boy.'

'I promise I won't wash for a month.'

'Well, with that fucking tongue of yours, Harry, you can come and shower with me anytime.' Her eyes said she meant it.

'Oh, I'd like that.' I meant it, too.

* * *

– Case #3 –

A SEX KITTEN FOR A CABINET MEETING

Then she got up and walked out of there. I never saw an ass like that in my life. Beyond concept. Beyond everything. Don't bother me now. I want to think about it.

- Charles Bukowski

A SEX KITTEN FOR A CABINET MEETING

– 1 –

Lying back in your birthday suit, with a barely legal young tart, also sensationally naked. Said young hussy has her mouth full, stretched wider than an anaconda swallowing a peccary, except in this case it's your ragingly hard cock.

There's a problem with this image: when it's photographed for posterity. Raises eyebrows in certain circles.

Say if one of the viewers is said tart's father.

Say if said father is a Cabinet Minister.

Say if said Cabinet Minister also happens to be your client.

As I said, there *is* a problem.

And so here I was, PI Harry Kenmare, good detective and even better libertine, sitting in the ministerial office of the Right Honourable Horace 'The Hammerhead' Stockland.

This man was a legend of Australian politics. He was slipperier than a greased pig, more cunning than a pack of foxes, and as ruthless as a shark, hence his moniker. His bullish, broad head with eyes set unusually far apart no doubt contributed. And that grin currently adorning his fat face was the epitome of malevolence. Especially as his chubby finger kept pointing out the said photo on an iPad.

How the fuck did he get it?

It was taken with a long telephoto lens: the compressed depth perspective gave that away. And it must have been through a window, although I couldn't for the life of me remember the precise layout of her lounge room. I'd been too busy getting my goanna gobbled to take in the décor.

My fault. Should never have gone back to her place, outside my territory. My brain had been saying, 'Control your environment, control the risks.' But it was a meek whisper compared to my cock yelling, 'The devil rides tonight!'

Cock versus brain? You know the rest.

– 2 –

Ten days ago, I'd been contacted by The Hammerhead's private secretary. The Minister had waited in the back seat of his car, whilst his effeminate, obsequious minion had a coffee with me a few metres away.

The Minister had heard his eighteen-year-old stepdaughter, Leona, was stripping. Given his ever-burgeoning political ambitions, if Leona's work was carnal and got out (and it would, eventually), then The Hammerhead's thus far superb and seemingly unstoppable rise towards the rank of State Premier could hit a monumental hurdle.

He needed her found, and persuaded to move interstate, without a whisper, never to return to Sydney.

An obviously warm and loving family.

Despite my visceral contempt for politicians, business is business, and I need plenty of cash to finance my own debauched lifestyle. Strippers and whores provide much of the colour and fun in my life. Cash is king.

Of course, the good Minister was going to pay premium rates. I had a hefty surcharge for politicians. And bankers. I called it my 'Establishment levy'. The irony appealed to my Irish blood.

The secretary gave me a card with a contact number, an envelope stuffed with cash for expenses, and a photo of Leona. The image was of her before her high school graduation ball, six months previously. She looked pretty damned hot, even allowing for the make-up and hairdo for the dance. She was almost busting out of the top of her ball gown: Leona had a veritable pair of melons. They'd be worth a close look, and more. Her young beau for the evening looked like a typical football team boofhead: bulging muscles, dull eyes, and no doubt an IQ to match his collar size. Still, I reckon he would've got his knob well and truly wet after the dance. If Miss Leona was out stripping already, she clearly wasn't a prude in the sex department. No, I reckon her virginity would have been a distant memory by now.

Before I left, the back window of the large Mercedes slid down and a fat ministerial finger summoned me.

I came within thirty centimetres of The Hammerhead's beady, bulging eyes.

'Do the job, Kenmare, and never say a word. Not even on your deathbed. Hear me?'

'Yep, no problems.'

'You deliver, keep silent, and you'll be very well paid.'

'Sounds good to me, Minister. One question.'

'What?'

'Why not have the cops find her? You've got enough mates in the senior ranks of the Force.'

He sniggered. I smelt last night's garlic and red wine. 'Because those wankers leak more than a tart's minge when the US Pacific Fleet's in town.'

Yeah, you couldn't argue that point about the city's finest. There was good reason their nickname was 'the best police force money can buy'.

– **3** –

My old detective days on the Vice Squad held me in good stead when it came to skulking in seediness. I tried a number of clubs of varying quality, but to no avail. Given how hot Leona was, she might have landed a top-shelf gig. Time to move on up.

The Purple Python was at the classier end of the market, referred to as a 'gentleman's exotic cabaret', rather than 'titty bar strip joint'. Whatever, it was still all tits and arses. Only the carnal quality determined an establishment's place on the class scale.

I was on my second scotch and dry, watered down for twice the normal price, seated next to the stage. The girls were all quality performers so far. There were two white girls: one looked Eastern European with those Slavic eyes and cheek-bones, and the other was an Aussie (got the broad local accent in the 'Thanks, mate' when I tucked some cash in her garter). There was a petite Thai girl with a huge rack, which was equally as firm when she hung upside down on the pole (you gotta love silicone), and one gorgeous African girl, again great breasts, one of those sensationally sculpted bottoms that seem on many African ladies to almost sit separately from their bodies, and a naughty smirk. I gave her some cash, too.

A couple of other girls had sauntered by, asking if I wanted a private show. I politely told them I wasn't ready for one yet. One thing the girls all had in common, apart from being infinitely fuckable, was the waft of that cheap, sweet, fruity perfume: 'Eau de Titty Bar'.

Two songs later, the lady of my quest made a superbly raunchy entry onto the stage. She'd looked seriously hot in her photo. In the flesh, she was smoking off the scale at twelve minimum. And to think I was getting paid for all this. I chuckled to myself.

Leona got into her moves, and was clearly a crowd favourite. Blokes were now occupying every seat next to the catwalk, and Leona's garter was garnering cash faster than the collection callout of a televangelist.

This was a bit like a card game. They were all sticking five- and ten-dollar notes in there. One half-pissed young buck stuck in a twenty as he made drunken eyes at her, probably imagining her as the future Mrs Young Buck.

Me, I'm an operator in these circles, nigh on an artiste.

Leona was down to her G string and parading on all fours, purring like a cat. I went for the artillery. I fished out a fifty. She was over in a flash, gyrating her torso and delicious breasts about ten centimetres from my face. The fifty went into her garter. As she leant down to say 'Thanks', I made my play.

'Love a private show with you, babe. I got a lot more pineapples in here.' I casually displayed my wallet and its yellow bundle of fifties.

She grinned. 'I'm all yours, handsome, as soon as I'm finished up here.'

'Cool.'

She gave me some more titty action and then headed for some other punters eager to stick their wages in her garter.

I was standing at the bar when Leona appeared by my side, smiling in her scarlet lingerie and peach-pink chiffon negligée. She now had a beautiful, red hibiscus flower pinned in her hair.

'A drink, babe?'

'Bubbles, please. But French,' she smiled.

'No other sort, is there?'

'Nope. I'm Kitty.' She held out her hand. 'Short for sex kitten.'

I took her hand. 'Yep, I can see that. I'm Harry. Short for here for a good time, not a long time.'

Her champagne arrived and she swallowed half the glass in one hit. The girl could drink. She was climbing in my estimation faster than a rat up a drainpipe.

'That's better. Thanks, Harry.'

'My pleasure.'

'So, the private show?'

'Absolutely. We good to go now?'

'Sure. Just buy me another champers and I'll get it arranged. Bring the drinks with you.' She kissed my cheek. And her perfume was Gaultier Classique, not the regulation fruity concoction. Good girl.

She walked off to the booking station at the end of the bar. I bought more drinks, then sauntered over. I paid for the half-hour private session, and away we went.

I sat on the plush bench seat as Kitty closed the smoked-glass door.

She sipped her champagne, put the glass down, slid off her negligée, and sashayed onto my lap. She was smiling wickedly, like a female Lucifer coming to plunder my soul (although Satan had missed the boat on that score). She dropped her bra, put her nose against mine, drowning me in her curly, blonde tresses. She breathed lustful tease all over me, purring gently. Then she pulled her head up, grabbed the back of mine, and buried my face in her voluptuous cleavage.

I'm not a religious man, quite the opposite in fact, but this was pretty close to heaven in my books. When I'd almost died a beautiful death of mammary suffocation, she leant back and smiled at me as she ground her crotch against the hard lump in my trousers.

'Now, sugar, for a hundred cash, without the boss out there knowing, you can touch me. But no pussy, just tits and arse. Sound good?'

I couldn't get the cash out of my wallet fast enough.

She tucked it away in her little purse next to her drink, and took another large sip. She stood up and removed her G string, twirled in front of me, and sat back on my lap. I wished it had been on my face. She ran her finger along her pussy and waved it under my nostrils. Ah, that unmistakeable aroma.

'*I* can touch my pussy, though,' she grinned at me as she stuck her finger into her mouth.

Damn, this girl was roasting hot.

Kitty smothered me with sensual bliss for twenty minutes, as I fondled every square centimetre of her magnificent breasts and her to-die-for derrière.

I let things proceed until I'd got my money's worth. As she eased off and asked me if I wanted another exorbitant half-hour, I got down to business.

'Babe, I'm also working right now.'

'Really? Good job you've got. How about you work at getting some more cash out of that fat wallet, sugar?'

She swished her hard nipples across my face, like a chastisement.

'Seriously, Kitty. Or should I say, Leona.'

She stopped moving.

'How the fuck do you know my name? You a fucking cop?'

'Not anymore. I'm a private investigator. Your stepfather hired me to find you and talk to you.'

Her lovely face turned vile.

'What the fuck does that cunt want?'

'Yeah, "cunt" does suit him. Can we talk after you finish? I will pay you well.'

She looked at me, considering the situation. I tapped the bulging wallet in my trouser pocket. The universal language in these environs.

'Okay. But not anywhere near here. We can find some place else to talk, and it'll cost you two hundred. If you want more than a chat, it'll be a thousand to spend the night with me.'

Fuck, this job got better by the minute. Despite her youth, this girl was no ingénue.

'I'll pay cash, baby. The sleep-over sounds great to me.'

She cracked a cheeky smirk. 'Well, if you want to sleep, that's your loss.'

I put my hand on her cheek, the one below her eye. 'Only after we're both exhausted, babe.'

'Good. Stick around and I'll let you know when I'm ready to go. Then I'll meet you outside.'

She bent down and kissed me on the lips, nice touch, and she was gone.

– 4 –

After my boner had subsided, I went back out to the main showroom and bought another drink. I stood at a tall table near the stage, watching the flesh parade and making sure I sipped slowly. My body needed to be up to the Leona challenge: a thousand bucks was going to involve a lot more than dirty conversation. And she was eighteen. She had a lot of physicality advantage over this middle-aged PI.

About fifteen minutes later, as I finished enjoying the Thai girl's latest dance, I turned around to peruse the crowd.

Leona was talking to a swarthy Arab at the end of the bar. She didn't look particularly happy. He looked as ugly as a hatful of arseholes.

The greasy dude grabbed Leona's arm, a bit too forcefully to be a client. This didn't feel right. I didn't like it.

But not out of jealousy: I hate seeing women victimized by men.

Sure, I love as much pussy as I can get, but always enthusiastically consensual.

A tall Slavic girl in lingerie, with a rack that would have converted Liberace to the straight team, brushed herself against me, smiling.

I couldn't help myself, I was smitten. 'God, you're beautiful, aren't you?' She was perfection personified.

She smiled at me, of course. 'So, handsome, private show with Tatiana?'

The Russian accent oozed sexuality, like a tube of KY being squeezed, and I started barring up again. Alas, duty called.

I smiled back at her, and discreetly indicated the slime-ball with Leona.

'Who's that man over there?'

Tatiana's inviting mien evaporated. Okay, so the slime-ball was somebody then.

'I … I can't say.' Her eyes dropped.

Time for my universal language skills again. I pulled my wallet out, slid out four fifties, folding them subtly, making my offer clear.

Tatiana looked around furtively, and her hand slid over mine, deftly removing the banknotes. The touch of her flesh felt sensational. Another time.

The cash disappeared in a flash into her underwear. I wanted to disappear in there myself.

She leant in and whispered, 'He is Mahmoud. Nephew of owner. Bad man. He hurts girls. I must go.'

I saw Leona pushed into a corridor leading away behind the bar. She looked scared. She caught sight of me as she disappeared.

I looked around for security. There were two thugs in dark suits near the door, that was it. But they'd sure see me when I headed for the corridor. And that is where I needed to go, pronto.

I looked around some more. There were two large young blokes sitting at the end of the catwalk, looking pretty well oiled. They were both muscled, suntanned, and wearing pressed chinos with R.M. Williams boots. Obviously farming lads here in the big smoke for a visit and sampling the specialities not likely available within hundreds of kilometres of their backwater home town out in the bush. I looked to their left and spotted a pair of bling-laden Turkish-looking guys. Time for some sport to give me some cover. I stepped over to the hayseed boys and tapped one of them on the shoulder, bending down as I did.

'Mate, you guys are country boys, aren't you?'

The big face breathed bourbon over me. 'Why the fuck ya' askin', pal?'

'Mate, relax. Just wanting to settle my curiosity. You see those two blokes over there?' I indicated the two olive-skinned stallions.

'What about 'em?' drawled the second bumpkin.

'They were having a good laugh. Said anyone dressed like you two had to be a pair of poofters.'

The farmers looked murderous and stood up.

I stepped back, sliding my trouble-making arse towards the bar.

'Oi, fuckstains!' the first farmer yelled at the Turks, who both looked surprised.

The second farmer joined in. 'Yeah, you two pretty boys. With all that jewelry, I reckon you two are the fuckin' poofters!'

'Yeah, you fuckin' wog cocksuckers,' added farmboy one.

And it was on: shouting, broken glasses, battle.

The goons by the door strode in and all attention was focused on the brawl.

I discreetly slipped past the bar and into the corridor.

A staircase was at the end. I climbed at a run, into darkness. One of those times I wished I'd been packing my trusty .38 Special, but I hadn't expected to need one in a strip joint. I got to the landing. There were three doors along a short hallway. Only one had light coming from underneath it. I could hear a man's voice, loaded with aggression. It was that condescending virulence of a man who was used to abusing women. Then I heard Leona yell, 'No!'

In I went.

The swarthy Leb turned to face me.

'Who the fuck are you?'

Leona was on a couch, ripped negligée on the floor along with her bra, her sensational tits back on display.

The bastard pulled a vicious-looking switchblade out of his trousers. The steel glinted in the light as the blade sprang forth.

Shit. I needed to claw back some advantage here. Best bet was to make him mad, cloud his fine-motor skills.

I pointed at Leona. 'Like picking on girls, do you? Makes you feel like a man? You fucking weak prick.'

He sneered at me. 'The bitch is mine. I'll do what I want to her. Now fuck off and mind your own business.'

Okay, Plan B.

'Mate, I suppose with your looks you need to force girls into it. I reckon when you slithered out of your mummy's cunt, you got a fair fucking flogging with the ugly stick. You really are one hideous Lebbo grease-ball.'

The sneer was replaced by narrowed eyes. 'I'll fucking kill you, arsehole.'

Progress. Finishing touches required.

'Mind you, back in Beirut or whichever Alibaba shithole you come from, your mummy probably took it up the arse from camels.'

There were no words this time, only a maniacal roar as he came at me, engulfed in rage for his slighted mother, and possibly the camel. Yes, reckoned that would do the trick.

Most of these macho Arab blokes are complete mummy's boys.

And given how manifestly ugly he was, I wondered whether maybe his mother had fucked a camel.

I let him get almost onto me, and I suddenly jumped to the left, grabbing his knife arm as he lunged wildly at me. I kicked his legs out from under him and he went down, me still holding his right forearm. I held his arm out straight and drove my foot into the back of his elbow. I heard the bone break. He howled like a Baghdad bitch.

With these scum, there is no such thing as a clean fight. You need to understand that to deal with them.

So, I sank my toecap into his face several times, breaking teeth and his nose. I then stood back and took a huge swing with my right leg, driving my foot into his crotch as if I was kicking for goal. Vomit followed the blood and tooth fragments coming out of his mouth, as he shrivelled into the foetal position. He wouldn't be getting up in a hurry.

Leona yelped, 'Behind you!'

I spun around to see a huge, dark Samoan or Tongan coming through the doorway. He obviously wasn't front-of-house staff given the gym gear he was wearing: baggy shorts, trainers, and a baseball singlet. And he was fucking built. I'd seen old-forest tree trunks slimmer than his thighs and his arms looked like Godzilla on steroids.

He lurched towards me, his bug-eyed face covered in malice. I let him get close and ducked. My right hand shot up the baggy leg of his shorts and I grabbed a pair of nuts the size of billiard balls. I squeezed and wrenched as if my life depended on it. It did.

He grabbed my head, which felt like being in a vice, but as I squeezed and twisted ever harder, his effort waned. He dropped to his knees, his face screwed up in the excruciating agony that goes with the ultimate direct assault on your manhood. Along with the pained expression, he was emitting a high-pitched whining. He looked and sounded like a Rottweiler shitting out a house brick. As he keeled over into the foetal position (this was turning into a maternity ward), I let go and withdrew my hand, desperately wanting to wash it. I was happy to smell of pussy, but sweaty scrotums were not my scene. Alas, time wouldn't allow.

'Go get your clothes and make it fast, babe, we need to get going.'

Leona scampered off down the stairs. I closed the door to wait.

Now, I know they say you shouldn't kick a man when he's down. They say all sorts of things: get a good job, marriage, mortgage, kids, second marriage, second mortgage, second job, nice steady run on the hamster wheel on the mundane road to death. But there are always exceptions to what they say.

And the two thugs lying moaning on the floor around me were A-grade exceptions. I sunk my toecap into both their gonads, twice, hard. The Leb vomited again (good effort, son). Neither of them was moving anytime soon.

Leona reappeared with a bag. She threw her street clothes on, and we headed out into the corridor. There was a fire escape door at its far end. I pushed hard on the release bar and the door swung outwards, onto a metal staircase. At the bottom, Leona took my hand and we ran out of the back lane onto George Street.

I hailed a taxi.

– 5 –

Leona gave the cabbie her address as soon as we were moving. I had been going to suggest my bachelor pad, my etching collection, and then rampant debauchery, but she got in first. Fine with me, debauchery could lay its sweet head anywhere in my books.

It was a short ride to her small apartment in Potts Point. I paid the driver and we went into one of those art deco blocks in need to some modern love.

We sat on her couch with cold beers.

'So, you wanted to talk to me?' she said, as she sat back against the armrest and ran her foot up the inside of my thigh.

Talk? I could think of a whole lot of better things to do right now, but best to get business out of the way first.

'Your stepfather, the good Minister …'

She interrupted me. 'The good fucking rapist, more like.'

I raised my eyebrows.

'That's right. I bet he didn't tell you he used to rape my older sister.'

'Nope. Did he …'

'No,' came back before I could finish. 'Amber always made sure he went for her instead of me. Right up until she was eighteen. Then one night she stepped off the platform at Central. I was sixteen. I knew he'd start on me then. And so I got out fast. Went to live with friends.'

'I'm sorry, Leona.' I stroked her foot.

'So, what does the lecherous old cunt want with me?'

'Reckons he's got wind of your working life and he's worried about his political future.'

She snorted. 'Fuck him. What the fuck do I care?'

'He wanted me to talk to you: negotiate you moving interstate, and making sure you use your mother's surname, not his.'

'I already do. Don't want any association with him.'

'He's willing to give you fifty grand, as long as you stay away from Sydney and he never hears from you, or of you.'

'Fifty, huh? I'll think about it. But first let me thank you for being my knight in shining armour tonight. That fucktard was going to hurt me.'

'My pleasure, babe. Always happy to help a lady, and I really hate fucktards.'

'Good combination, we could be friends,' she purred as she crawled over to me, placing a hand on my crotch and her lips on mine.'

'I like the sound of friends,' I whispered over her invading tongue.

'So, how exactly would you like your thank you?'

'Every way imaginable.'

She grinned. Her hand extracted my raging boner from my pants. She stroked the head of my cock.

'Strip,' she commanded, as she stood up and shed her clothes.

I peeled off quicker than the Marquis de Sade in a convent.

'Lie down.'

I obeyed. I closed my eyes in ecstasy as she rolled her tongue around my glans. She had expertise this young lady. She took my shaft into her mouth.

After a minute, she disengaged and stood, holding out her hand.

'Let's hit the bed, big boy.'

'Take me away, sex kitten!'

We fell apart after a torrid and sweaty couple of hours: seven orgasms, four hers, three mine. She'd taken me everywhere. Dirty and gorgeous. She went and got us more cold beers from her fridge. As she was in the kitchenette, I noticed a framed quote on the chest of drawers, next to her make-up mirror.

"In the depths of winter I found that there lay
within me an invincible summer."

Bloody hell. A chick who was beautiful, sexually wild, and liked Albert Camus. If I were the marrying sort …

But I'm not. Been there, got the scars. And zero assets.

She came back in and handed me a beer.

I took a swig as she sat down. I indicated the quote.

'I'm a big fan of Camus.'

'Yeah, me too from the little I've read. I found that quote after Amber died. It spoke to me. I know she'd want me to find the summer she never had.'

I gave her a hug.

She smiled at me. There was a glint of mischief in her sultry eyes. 'Hey, how about a little game?'

'Babe, I'd love to, but you have fucking drained me, literally.'

She poked me in the ribs. 'Not more sex. Not yet, anyway. No, an acting game.'

I frowned. 'You mean like charades?'

'Sort of. You're a PI, so you got one of those nifty little recorders?'

'Sure have, always carry one. It's in my jacket.'

'Can I?'

'Sure.'

I admired her exquisite derrière wiggling as she walked over to the chair in the lounge room I'd draped my jacket over. She reached into the pocket and came back with my digital voice recorder.

I frowned again as she handed it to me.

'And you used to be a cop, right?'

'Yeah.'

'Interview any rape victims?'

'Yes, several.'

'Good. So, you're the copper and I'm the rape victim. Listen to my idea.'

I listened, and I smiled. This girl was so smart I was in danger of getting attached to her.

I pressed 'Record' and we started our game.

– 6 –

The Right Honourable Hammerhead beamed triumphantly at me.

'Well, Kenmare, don't reckon I'll be paying the rest of your fucking outrageous bill, let alone any bonus.'

You cunt, is what I thought. Nothing is what I said.

'Had another gumshoe watching her place from the building across the road. But he wasn't getting anything useful, so I hired you for the more direct approach. And now, my randy little friend, here we are.'

Okay, so it had been a telephoto shot from outside. Glad the bedroom curtains had been closed, or the photos would have been unspeakable.

'Come off it, Stockland, I did the job for you.'

'It's "Minister" to you, arsehole. Now, you can relay to the little slut that I'll transfer the money to her account as soon as I get confirmation she's left Sydney. And you, my friend, aren't getting another single, fucking cent. Any complaints and I'll have a chat with my good friend, the Police Commissioner. Your PI licence will become a minor footnote to the sorry history of the Sydney security industry. I'll squash you, Kenmare.'

His smile was the ugliest mixture of smug and vicious I'd ever seen.

Righto, fight-back time.

'I don't think so, *Minister*.' I heaped contempt onto that last word.

He looked at me incredulously. 'Who the fuck do you think you are?'

I pulled out my trusty voice recorder and pressed 'Play'. A girl's voice spoke.

> 'My name is Amber Stockland, eighteen years of age, and I am making this statement to Detective Sergeant Smith. My stepfather, Horace Stockland, the politician, has been raping me since I was fifteen …'

And Leona went on, and on, gruesomely describing the repeated violation of Amber by the Right Honourable member. Leona had assured me her voice was almost indistinguishable from that of her late, older sister.

The voice continued.

> 'Horace always pulled out of my vagina and ejaculated in my bottom. He told me it was so I wouldn't get pregnant.'

The good Minister had gone paler than an Aryan Nation poster boy. It was wonderful to see such arrogance so utterly crushed.

'Enough!' He banged his desk. 'You … That can't … That little tart's dead!'

'Yeah, so?'

'You've … You've cooked this up with Leona. And I never touched Leona.'

'Maybe not. But you fucked Amber until she killed herself.'

His smile crept back, tentatively to start, and then malignantly, like mustard gas rolling over no man's land.

'Exactly, so she can't testify. And that piss-weak fabrication of yours won't get near a court.'

'Horace, *mate*, it doesn't need to. In this day and age, I'll just stick this on social media. Truth, fake news, whatever. No one really gives a fuck anymore. Your reputation will be finished. The average voters might be blasé these days about extramarital affairs or expense rorting: they're almost mandatory for you politicians. You'd survive those minor scandals.'

I paused, to add dramatic effect to my smirk.

'But arse-fucking your fifteen-year-old stepdaughter? No, no, no. That, *mate*, is still a political dead-end.'

I increased my grin.

He glared at me. 'What does the little slut want?'

'She is going to move cities, as you've requested, but you're going to give her two hundred and fifty thousand. And that photo of me and her never sees the light of day. We have a classic Mexican stand-off. It'll keep us both honest. Oh, and you *will* pay my bill, naturally.'

The steam coming out of his ears was almost visible. He said nothing.

'We got a deal, *Horace*?'

'Yes,' he hissed. 'But you double-cross me, I'll fuck you over until you wished you'd been gang raped by the Hells Angels.'

'Ouch, Horace, that's not very nice coming from a Minister of the Crown. No reason for me to renege on the deal, it works for both of us. Text me when you've transferred the money to Leona, and to me.'

I stood.

'I'll see myself out.'

I walked to the door and opened it. I stepped through, but leant my head back in.

'Oh, and by the way, the part on the recording where Amber gives such a graphic description of being arse-fucked? Know why it sounds so realistic? I was chock-a-block up Leona's arse as she uttered those words. Bye!'

I closed the door in the nick of time: a glass object shattered on its inside.

Time to go and celebrate the victory.

With Leona, of course!

* * *

– Case #4 –

THE LONELY CORPSE

I wanted Virginia, she was a creature of moonlight, crazy as moonlight, all upthrusting radiance and hard silver dimples and hollows, built for one thing and only one thing and perfectly for that.

- Elliott Chaze

THE LONELY CORPSE

– 1 –

She was standing outside my office door: fretful, indecisive, uncertain. Clearly in need of help. Like a furtive adolescent outside the VD clinic, for the first time.

The young woman was dowdy, with plain clothes and no make-up. Unlike Terri I'd taken home from the pub last night. Plenty of make-up, and then no clothes. The reason I was late this morning. Pretty sure her name was Terri. Totally sure the sex was awesome.

I coughed lightly as I approached. The plain girl lifted her face. She had timid, doleful eyes, but a lovely amber colour: unusual and exotic.

'I'm Harry Kenmare, Private Investigator.' I switched my coffee into my left hand and held out my right. She took it tentatively.

'Sylvie. Sylvie Wells.'

'Pleased to meet you, Sylvie. I'm normally in before now. I hope you haven't been waiting too long.'

'A little while. But that's fine. I didn't know what else to do.'

I unlocked my door.

'Come on in.' I ushered her into my tatty office and motioned her into the client chair in front of my desk.

I sat down. She glanced nervously around the office, like a refugee arriving in a camp.

As I sipped my coffee, I gave her top half the once over. Those amber eyes were lovely, and her full lips were inviting, despite their paleness. Her chestnut hair was cut in a bob and looked like a home job. Her nose was a little small for her face, but cute in a pixie way. She wore a tight, pastel-green blouse that stretched over her ample breasts. Make-up and a hairdresser would do wonders.

She clutched her scuffed, brown-leather handbag as if it were a safety blanket. Her eyes settled on me.

I took a moment to stare into them. She was an ingénue, this one. I didn't get to meet too many of her ilk in my life, either personally or professionally.

'So, Sylvie, what do you need a PI for?'

'It's a bit of a long story. My great-aunt died.' She paused.

'How much do you charge, Mister Kenmare?'

'That varies. And it's Harry, please.'

'Okay, Mister … Sorry, Harry. But I don't have much money.'

Her unpractised eyes gave a shot at the damsel-in-distress look. She got halfway there. Far enough for me to feel a twinge.

Usually bring me trouble, those twinges. But life's here to be lived, not endured.

'Why don't you tell me the story and then we can see about what I might charge.'

'Okay, thank you.' She cleared her throat delicately. 'Aunty Ethel was my only close family member left. My grandparents have all passed away.' She paused again.

'And my parents were killed in a car accident three years ago. I don't have any brothers or sisters.'

'I'm sorry. And you've no other relatives at all?'

'Well, there is Uncle Walter, but we're not in contact. I've never really had anything to do with him. He was always at extended family events, invited out of a sense of duty, I think. But he wasn't ever left alone with any of the kids, if you understand?'

'Oh, yes. I used to be a cop. Met quite a few of Uncle Walter's type.'

'And there are some distant cousins. Anyway, after Mum and Dad died, Aunty Ethel had some money they'd left her, to look after me in case anything ever happened to them. And so Aunty sent me to a convent in Spain to become a nun. Aunty was very religious. I was only twenty at the time.'

'Hell, that must've been a shock.'

'Not really. I had a sheltered childhood. I think that's the polite term for it.'

'You're not wearing a nun's outfit now?'

She went ever so slightly red, like the early glow of a sunset on the underside of clouds. A hint of a smirk warmed her face further.

'There was an "incident", as the sisters called it. I was asked to leave the convent. Which was fine with me. I didn't really fit it. I'd stayed to keep Aunty happy. So, I didn't tell her and stayed in Madrid with a friend's family. Anyway, one day early last month a letter arrived, forwarded on from the Mother Superior. It was from the family solicitor here to let me know Aunty had died. I came straight back. I knew she'd been ill: she'd told me. But I didn't realize she was bedridden, and I thought her granddaughter, my cousin, was looking after her. It seems cousin Natasha has a drug problem and took all Aunty's money and things. It's so awful.'

She sighed, and resumed. 'The solicitor put me in touch with the police who found her. The neighbours had complained about the smell. They reckon she hadn't been fed in weeks and had run out of water by her bed. She died all alone.'

She looked back into her lap.

'I'm very sorry, Sylvie.'

'Damned Natasha didn't even have the decency to show up for the funeral.'

'So, why an investigator?'

'I've inherited Aunty's house in Newtown. She'd told me she would be leaving it to me. She made comments about Natasha, so I think she was wise to her problems. Aunty also said her family jewelry would be mine. But it's all gone. The policeman said when they went into the house, there was nothing much left.'

'That figures.'

'The place had been stripped of anything remotely valuable. Just the beds and some old furniture left, and Aunty's clothes and stuff. TV, record player, radio, all gone. Even the fridge and washing machine.'

'Yeah, junkies. I've seen these situations before. Always like this.'

'I want to see if there's anything we can do about the family jewels. I'm not interested in their money value, I want them for sentimental reasons. It's all that's left, apart from memories. There's one piece in particular. A ruby brooch that Aunt's grandmother had passed down to her.'

'You realize your cousin has probably sold it all by now?'

'But I have to try. Please?'

The puppy-dog look was back in her eyes as she stopped talking and looked at me.

Oh, what the fuck. It would be only a few enquiries and then a dead-end. The jewels would be lost to the pawnbroker-managed network of stolen goods, never to be seen again.

'All right, Sylvie. I'll take the job.'

A smile blossomed on her face. It transformed her. 'Thank you, Harry. But what about your fee?'

'We'll discuss that later. Why don't we go and check out your Aunty's house?'

'Great.'

'Tell me to mind my own business if you want, but I'm curious as to this "incident" at the nunnery?'

The peach colour warmed her face again. As did that cute smirk.

'There was another girl,' she almost whispered. 'The incident was one night when I made too much noise. But I couldn't help myself. We were discovered.'

I grinned. 'My curiosity is satisfied.'

She chuckled. 'Yes, so was I, that was the problem.'

Okay, so she wasn't a complete innocent. And she had a sense of humour. I was already feeling better about doing the job pro bono.

At that moment, the door opened and in walked Tanya, my assistant and regular lover. I did often ask myself how a drop-dead-stunning nymphomaniac in her twenties persisted, amongst other dalliances, with me. But I never pondered too long. *C'est la vie.* The two young women looked at each other. Tanya introduced herself. I spotted a gleam in Sylvie's eyes.

Okay, Harry, get your mind out of the gutter and back to work.

I gave Tanya the low-down of the new case. She grinned at me: knew me too damned well.

'Let's go visit the house, Sylvie. See if we can find anything useful.'

'Thanks so much, Harry.' She stood up. She and Tanya shook hands again. There was a hint of a lingering.

I led Sylvie out and hailed a taxi on George Street.

– 2 –

The cab dropped us out the front of a run-down, single-storey, dark-brick house a stone's throw from the Camperdown Memorial Park. The view of the old cemetery was sadly apt. Aunt Ethel's house was one of the few stand-alone places in the street and once would have been a cosy inner suburban home. Now it was a candidate for a renovation project for some yuppie couple. Or more likely in Sydney these days, a target for the wrecking ball of some arsehole property developer.

Whilst its former resident was now deceased, there was one original survivor in the small front garden. A large frangipani tree was in full, magnificent bloom, the sea of white and yellow flowers thumbing their collective nose at any remodelling to come. In the still, hot air, the delicate fragrance wafted over us as Sylvie opened the front door.

I stepped over the threshold and a wholly different waft enveloped me. Even the onslaught of cleaning-chemical fumes couldn't entirely mask the background whiff. To the untrained nose it would have seemed maybe a rodent had died under the floorboards. But I knew that smell all too well: the reek of putrefaction when a human corpse sweltered in the Australian summer. Back in my days as a constable, and attending these unpleasant calls,

I'd had to burn my uniform once because the smell was so stubborn.

'The cleaning company told me it'd be a few weeks at least for the smell to go completely,' said Sylvie. She closed the door behind me.

'This was Aunty's room.' She led me into the main bedroom.

The bed was made and a number of photos and other personal items were laid out on it. It resembled a makeshift shrine.

She touched my arm. 'An effort at a memorial. At least with what's left after Natasha cleaned her out.'

'I take it you had the locks changed?'

'Yes. The police suggested that.'

She sat on the edge of the bed, picking up a sepia-toned photo in an old, pewter frame and showing it to me. A serious woman, formidable in that universal, old-fashioned photo pose, stared at me coolly.

'Aunty could be hard, but she was a good person. I can't bear to think of her lying here alone and dying slowly.'

'Yeah, I remember now the story in the newspaper when they found her. It is awful. No one should go like that.'

'I hate Natasha!' she yelled. 'I fff … I really hate her.' She started sobbing.

I sat next to her and put my arm around her shoulders. Her inability to launch the expletive was artless and endearing: not common features in the company I kept. She took hold of my free hand and held it in her lap.

'Loneliness is the most terrible poverty,' she said.

'Sadly profound.'

'One of Mother Teresa's sayings. We learnt lots of them at the convent.'

'I've never been into religion myself. I'm an avowed heathen. I like it that way.'

She turned and a slight grin brightened her face, dismissing the glumness. 'Sounds naughty.'

I laughed. 'Yeah. Sounds like living life to me. I enjoy it.'

She looked into my eyes.

I could feel the pulse in her hand. And the one in my groin. 'I was thinking of a line from one of my favourite books: "There's no greater misfortune than dying alone." Similar sentiment to yours.'

'Which book?'

'*Memories of my Melancholy Whores*, by Gabriel García Márquez. A magnificent author.'

She pondered for a moment. 'Do you think whores are melancholy?'

I chuckled. Unexpected question. 'Some maybe. Others definitely not.'

'Do you know any whores?'

Now that was a bit more predictable. 'I think of them as working women. And, yes, I do.'

She kept looking at me. 'I see.'

She stood up, a slight grin loitering. 'I'll leave you to look around and see if you can find any clues, or whatever it is detectives look for.'

She dug into her purse and handed me a card. 'This is the policeman I dealt with. Maybe you can call him.'

'Okay. I'll do that and have a look around.'

She smiled and walked out.

I didn't know what to make of this girl.

I rang the cop's number. I knew Sergeant Dario Trivoli from my days back in the job many years before.

'Dario? Harry Kenmare.'

'Well, bugger me. Harry, it's been years. How's the gumshoe life treating you?'

'All good, mate. Can't complain. And no fucker listens anyway. How's the Force?'

He chortled. 'Mate, the job's still fucked. And getting worse. So, to what do I owe the pleasure?'

I told him I was on the Aunt Ethel case. He filled me in on how they'd found her after a neighbour's call. The pathologist said Ethel had been dead for at least a fortnight before she was found. Cause of death had been dehydration leading to organ failure. After whoever was caring for her stopped visiting, her immobility had meant once the jug of water on the bedside table was empty, it was a slow, painful few days until death. The cops had thought it strange there was nothing at all of value in the house, but had no leads to indicate any foul play. The case had been closed as a sudden death of natural causes.

I thanked Dario and rang off.

I had a poke around the room: in the wardrobe and drawers, checked for loose floorboards, lifted the mattress, looked behind the two faded, framed pictures on the walls. Nothing of interest.

The heat in the house was almost tropical. I went out into the hall.

'Sylvie?'

No answer. No noise at all.

I looked into the sitting-room, but it was empty.

The next room was the second bedroom. As I turned my head to look in, I was greeted by one of my most favourite of sights: a naked woman.

Sylvie was lying on her side on the single bed, head propped up on her hand. It wasn't often anything stopped me in my tracks, but this was a genuine surprise.

Yep, those breasts were ample, and looked as firm as two giant marshmallows. Her body was a creamy colour, like ivory, and she was hairless. Except for her crotch: another clue to her unworldliness. Her bush was dense and untamed, reminiscent of a 1970s *Playboy* centrefold. Brazilian was clearly still only a nationality in Sylvie's vocab. And it'd been a long time since I'd forged my way through a jungle like that: Doctor Livingstone territory, and call me 'Stanley'.

She attempted to pout. It came across as comely. Blood was surging in my crotch.

I walked over and sat on the bed. She grabbed my hand and manoeuvred it onto her breast. Firm was an understatement. And the nipple was like a pebble.

'Take me. Take me for your fee.'

I smiled at her. I'd never considered pro bono in this light before. 'You don't have to do this, Sylvie. I'm doing the job for you for free.' However, I couldn't quite resolve to take my hand off her sweet breast.

'Then just take me anyway. I've never had a man inside me. I want to experience that, and you seem a decent man.'

Yeah, I wasn't getting into that discussion.

When you look up 'decent' in the dictionary, my name doesn't feature heavily. Not even in the urban version.

She sensed my hesitation. 'You do like me, don't you, Harry?'

'Of course, Sylvie, you're lovely.' And I meant it. Her young, naked body lying there was delectable. And available.

'So, what's the problem then?' She did her best to look slighted. That was charming, too.

'I don't believe in taking advantage of people.'

The mischievous little smile returned. 'You won't be.' The background odour evidently hadn't restrained Sylvie's libido. 'I really do want this,' she purred.

And with that she slid my hand off her breast, slowly down her flat, taut stomach, and pushed it into her crotch as she parted her thighs.

'Make love to me, Harry. Now.'

Her sex was sodden with juices, like a rain forest after a deluge. I suspected she'd worked on herself whilst waiting for me to find her.

The look in her eyes now was far away from ingénue. Sylvie was a wanton woman. And here I was. What to do?

I gave her vagina a light squeeze and floated my hand back towards my face. I could smell her well before I licked my fingers.

Hell, she was strong. Some women have incredibly pungent pussies, and Sylvie reeked. Damn, it turned me on.

'I should warn you, Sylvie, I eat pussy like a wild animal. And it's mandatory.'

'Well, I know I like that part. I used to love Eva doing it to me in the convent.'

My raging erection made getting undressed a little more awkward than usual, and Sylvie gasped as I turned to face her, naked. I think it was her first phallic encounter. She looked mesmerized and agape, like a child admiring the window display of a toy shop. But the hand that grabbed my rod was every bit woman.

She swung her legs off the bed so she was sitting and pulled me towards her. She hugged my cock against her cheek making a cooing noise. I ran my fingers through her hair. She kissed the tip of my glans before sliding her mouth over my pulsing head. Despite her novice status on the penis front, she was careful with her teeth and her tongue stroked the underside of my member. Fuck, that felt good.

Well, when doesn't it?

But there was a more pressing priority. I eased her head back and my cock sprang upwards out of her mouth, clipping the end of her nose. She giggled.

'Do you want me to continue? I'm happy for you to ejaculate in my mouth.'

Her textbook terminology was quaint.

'All in good time, my beautiful Sylvie. First, my tongue has an urgent appointment with your pussy.'

She giggled again. 'Oh, yes. I was forgetting. Silly me. I'm all yours.'

She lay back and I got onto the bed. I was going to kiss her first, but with both hands she propelled my head southwards. I pushed her silky thighs even further apart and dived into her steaming vaginal valley.

The pungency would have daunted a visitor who wasn't a cunnilingus connoisseur, but I was hooked. This was ambrosial. My tongue got to work, delving between her labia and massaging her clitoris.

I've heard men complain about odorous women, but I reckon they're the self-centred males who don't care for pleasing women anyway. Selfish pricks.

Me? The piscine redolence was pure aphrodisiac. I licked and probed and sucked and nibbled for about ten minutes, the noises from above becoming more sonorous and urgent. Finally, Sylvie spasmed as if she'd been electrocuted. And she hollered. I wondered if the neighbours would be on the phone about a screaming orgasm as readily as a decaying body. I kept teasing her lightly with my tongue until she giggled, pushing my head away. 'No more, Harry, I can't take it.'

Ah, music to my ears: the perfect coda to my cunnilingual efforts.

Liquid had dribbled down her thighs and I wiped my face thoroughly in it.

I slid along her body until her lips hungrily locked on to mine. Fortunately my tongue still had some reserves of energy. It needed them.

'Get inside me, please, Harry.'

'Are you …'

'Don't worry,' she interrupted. 'I'll see the doctor tomorrow. Hurry up! I want it, now!'

Don't they say the client is always right? I wasn't going to pick this precise moment to argue.

I guided my cock in between her labia and eased all the way inside her. She was warm, and tight, and wet. And I groaned, it felt so awesome.

Sylvie had wrapped her arms around me and was laughing like a lunatic.

'Oh, yes, yes. Oh, Harry.' She kept repeating this mantra.

The madcap cackling and the verbal encouragement continued for the few minutes I was able to hold out for before exploding inside her.

My shout of ecstasy didn't compete with hers, but it was voluble all the same. I rolled off her after a minute and she turned to rest her face on my shoulder.

'Thank you.'

'My pleasure, believe me.'

'Mine, too. That was fun. Do you know other ways of doing it as well?'

'I do have something of a repertoire, yes.'

'Maybe you could show me some as the case goes on? You know, I do need to pay your fees.' She giggled at her own joke.

'I'm sure that can be arranged.'

She hummed happily on my chest.

'By the way, talking of the case, I've got some photos.'

She reached for her purse on the bedside table and opened it, pulling out an envelope. It contained five photos of jewelry. There were two necklaces: one a string of pearls, and one a gold chain with a topaz pendant. Next a pair of pearl earrings, which matched the necklace. Then a diamond and sapphire ring. But the last photo stole the show. The piece was in the design of a large beetle with a gold head and legs, and the body was a hulking, blood-red ruby. It had to be at least three centimetres long, judging by the dollar coin at the side of the each picture, to provide scale. It would be worth an absolute packet.

She tapped the photo.

'Find my beetle, Harry.'

I didn't feel up to dampening the mood by reminding her of the likely futility.

'I'm on the case, babe.'

'Good. Now, show me another way of doing it.'

'Yes, boss.' I rolled her onto her stomach.

– 3 –

It's not hard to set a trap for a junkie. Anything that'll pay for their next hit will do, cash or convertibles. Like flies to shit.

'I hate her, but I don't want her hurt,' implored Sylvie. 'Can you find the jewels without hurting her?'

'Sylvie, let me explain a few things about junkies …'

Tanya cut me off. 'Sylvie, look at it this way,' she said, putting her arm around the girl's shoulders. 'You loved your great-aunt. She loved you, in her own style. She wanted you to have the jewels because she knew exactly what Natasha is like. And remember that love when you think about how Natasha treated her, stole from her, and then left her to die. Alone.'

Sylvie burst into tears and buried her face into Tanya's chest.

Tanya and Trev had arrived a few minutes earlier. The trap needed a team, plus transport. Trev had the wheels, his trusty VW surveillance van, and I needed Tanya for the physical part of persuading Natasha to talk. I was more comfortable with her doing that side of things: gratuitous belting of females didn't sit well with me, self-defence excepted. When I'd explained Natasha's behaviour to Tanya, she'd had no hesitation in volunteering to inflict some pain for a good cause: she hated predators of either gender.

Tanya took Sylvie off to the kitchen at the back of the house, before returning to the lounge room. She had a huge grin on her face.

'What?' I asked.

'Hey, Trev,' said Tanya. 'You should go and sniff the spare bedroom. Our Harry here has been taking customer service to *extreme* levels.'

Trev slapped me on the shoulder. 'You fucking rogue, Kenmare.'

'Yeah, bet she'd never had that sort of service at the convent.' Tanya poked me in the ribs. 'Still, good to know she's up for it. I rather fancy a go myself.'

'Bloody hell, you two,' said Trev. 'Can we focus on work, for a change?' He smiled.

Tanya blew him a kiss. 'Ooh, the green-eyed monster speaks.'

We all had a laugh.

'All right,' I said. 'Babe, you know what Sylvie needs to say on the phone?'

'Yep. Tell bitch Natasha to get her skanky arse round here because Sylvie's found a hidden envelope with cash and Natasha's name on it. Then the trap is set.'

Trev chuckled. 'Love it. So easy with junkies. Like stealing candy from a baby.'

Tanya left the room.

Less than an hour later, I watched through the heavy, lace curtains of the front room as a skinny woman in her late twenties turned in off the street. She might have been attractive once, but she'd injected her way into ugliness. Her face was pale and drawn, and her hair looked like a mop head fresh out of a bucket of dirty water.

She put a key into the lock, and looked confused when it didn't work. She jabbed at the doorbell.

I watched Sylvie walk past in the hallway. I heard the front door open.

'Hello, Natasha.'

'Sylvie.' The voice was verging on gravel. Obviously heading down the same ugly gutter as her looks: riding the needle all the way to hell.

'Come in. I'll put the kettle on.'

The door closed.

'Fuck coffee, cuz. Got any vodka?'

I listened to the two sets of footsteps padding along the hall to the kitchen.

'Might have. I'll check the cupboard.'

A rancid body odour floated in from the hall. Guess regular showering wasn't as high on Natasha's list as getting the next fix. And judging from the edginess in her voice, she was badly in need.

I tiptoed down the passage with Trev behind me. Exactly as planned, Natasha was sitting at the table, back towards us. And right on cue, Tanya came in from the laundry out the back.

Natasha stood up. 'Who the fuck are you?'

'Friend of Sylvie's,' said Tanya. As she stepped over to the junkie, she pulled her arm back and delivered a beautiful right hook smack bang into Natasha's face. The junkie staggered backwards, into the chair, and went arse over. Tanya was on her in a flash, pinning her to the floor on her stomach.

I stooped down and put cable ties around Natasha's wrists and ankles. I dragged her up by her jacket collar and sat her back in her chair that Trev had righted.

'Who the fuck are you cunts?' spluttered Natasha through snot and tears.

Trev flicked open a switchblade about thirty centimetres in front of her face. Fear shot across her strung-out eyes.

I leant in, but not too close. I'd been spat on by junkies when I was a copper, and I'd learnt the right proximity. Waiting for test results for hepatitis C reinforces those lessons.

'Doesn't matter who we are, you junkie slag. You're going to answer some questions.'

'Fuck off, pig. Think I can smell bacon.'

Trev waved the blade closer to her. 'We look like pigs to you? Really? And the only stench around here is you, you filthy little skank. From here your armpits smell awful enough, I dread to think how bad it is inside your pants. Been a long time since your festering cunt would have seen a bar of soap.'

The blade now rested on her cheek, the point depressing the skin. Natasha obviously decided another smart-arse reply wasn't such a good idea: a wet patch spread around the crotch of her grubby jeans.

I turned to Sylvie. 'This might get unpleasant, a bit more physical, so if you want to wait in the lounge?'

She nodded her head, looking worried: her naïve view of the world and the creatures that lurked within it. She left the kitchen.

I turned back to our captive. 'So, Natasha, you're going to tell us where the jewels are that you took from here.'

'Don't know what you're fucking talking about.'

The odour from her halitosis was as putrid as her BO. Her breath smelt somewhere between a dero who'd drunk a four litre flagon of cheap port and an ageing terrier that'd just finished off a bone it'd dug up.

'Oh, dear. The attitude is back,' said Trev.

'Indeed it is. Now, Natasha, you fucking little slag, when we *were* both pigs, we used to assess how to treat people on the basis of the attitude test, as we called it. Whether they passed or failed.'

'And you're failing big time, girlie,' said Trev, tracing the point of his knife blade across her face. He pushed the point into her chin, puncturing her skin as she shrieked. A drop of blood formed as he withdrew the blade.

He smiled at her. 'Plenty more where that came from, girlfriend, if you want to play tough.'

'I … I don't …' She couldn't even utter more of her own bullshit. I stood back and nodded at Tanya. Trev moved back as well.

Tanya stepped in and drove her fist into Natasha's guts. Fuck, I would've been proud of that one. There wasn't a single day I didn't find something to admire about Tanya. And that was on top of her smarts and her looks.

The sudden expulsion of air from the fetid girl simply increased the fug of decaying gums. Good job Natasha was the typical junkie who didn't eat regularly, or her last meal would have emptied forth from her.

Tanya pulled on a dishwashing glove, grabbed a handful of Natasha's soiled hair, and jerked her head back up from between her knees.

'Happy to do a whole lot more, honey. You want to play with me?'

The girl squealed as Tanya twisted her hair and pulled backwards. Then she let go.

Natasha's face came forward again, now streaked with tears.

'At my place,' she wheezed.

Tanya snatched the hair again.

'Where at your place exactly? And where is your place?'

'Dwayne. He'll kill me.'

'Not if I do first.' Tanya twisted the hair again. Natasha whimpered.

Trev held a sachet of white powder up in front of her.

She tried to focus her eyes through her tears.

Trev wiggled the packet. 'Good girls get a lolly.'

A glimmer lit up her jaded eyes. 'Please, yes, anything.' Clearly her need outweighed her fear of Dwayne.

She gave us the address and details of the stash spot where the jewels were. She said they hadn't got rid of them yet as their usual fence wasn't around. They were waiting for him.

We let her shoot up and as she lolled into her reverie, Trev hit her with a dose of chloroform. Out she went.

As did we, walking the sleeping Natasha out between myself and Tanya, as if she were a drunk friend, and into the van for our mission.

I told Sylvie to stay put and then to meet us at my office when I called her, hopefully with her jewels.

– 4 –

The junkies' house was an ancient, dilapidated, weatherboard bungalow in Mascot. It was a total shithole, as you'd expect from the likes of Natasha and crew, the tenants from hell. But it did have one piece of charm, arguably: it was one of the few houses left, amongst the burgeoning jungle of shoddily built apartment blocks. It was like a mange-ridden mouse running through a pen full of pigs.

The modern version of Sydney is geared to suit only three groups of people, none of which are Joe Citizen, who has to live, at an exorbitant cost, in this concrete abomination. No, the twenty-first century in Sydney is all about corrupt property developers, corrupt politicians and councillors, and corrupt bankers. I guess not so different from much of the Western world. It's an easy equation of greased palms and offshore bank accounts that leads to a housing market where quality sinks to the lowest common denominator, and average citizens consign themselves to a lifetime of debt.

It's the serfdom of the modern age.

Trev reversed the van into the overgrown driveway at the side of the house, stopping short of an old, rusty Datsun 120Y with flat tyres and more cobwebs than the spider house at the zoo. Parking in the drive wasn't ideal, possibly being seen there, but we needed to unload the unconscious Natasha, and from the driveway was easier than from the street.

We sat in the van for a couple of minutes, listening.

Zilch.

The front of the hovel was boarded up. Looked as if it was going to be a back door job. And not of the erotic variety.

'Okay, team, let's do this,' I said.

Trev opened the gun-box, handed me my trusty .38 Special, and a five-shot model to Tanya. She had settled on the smaller piece as her comfortable equalizer of choice, at least when circumstances allowed for a choice. Trev grabbed his usual .357 Ruger.

He grinned. 'Back in business. Love this team: all tooled up, and ready to party.'

We put on cotton gloves and exited via the van's rear door, leaving Natasha out cold, tied and gagged.

I led the way past the vintage Datto and round the back. The flyscreen door was lying on what had once passed as lawn. Now it looked more like a slab of the Sahara. The back door itself was hanging open.

I pulled my gat out and slunk up the two steps and in through the doorway.

The stench was appalling: like eau-de-Natasha sprayed liberally around. It was an infernal mixture of urine, body odour, and rotting garbage, overlaid with a chemical tinge of burnt opiates.

I went forward, .38 raised and ready. If you want to meet unpredictability on two legs, try a junkie. Especially one who's hanging for it.

Through the kitchen at the back. Clearly not much edible cooking done in this house. But there was no shortage of saucers and spoons with the dark treacle residue on them. And a dozen ciggie lighters lying around.

I peered into the lounge room. I could see a male head, shaved and dog-fucking ugly, lolling against the headrest of an armchair. He had an inane smile on his face and a dribble of saliva hung from the corner of his mouth.

Next as I turned I was greeted by a pair of buttocks, definitely female (I knew my repertoire in that scene), with the top of the body hidden by the back of the old, brown, vinyl couch. All I got was the bottom end, legs draped down to the floor. I reckoned she'd been done doggy-style over the arm of the couch, and stayed there.

I stepped in, feeling Trev's breath right behind me.

If there's one time you do want to feel hot breath on your neck, and when it's not a lusty woman, it's when you're going into action and need to know your offsider has your back.

My .38 still at the ready, I closed in on the female posterior, normally a manoeuvre I relished, but not like this. The male druggie in the armchair was off with the fairies, so no problem there.

As I approached the female butt cheeks, I saw the parted thighs and the cum trails running from her pussy. Then I saw her comatose face, seventeen or eighteen I guessed, pressed against the dirty couch, and the needle hanging out of the inside crease of her elbow. The tourniquet was still in place.

A private-school blazer and matching skirt lay over the other end of the couch. A school bag, similarly badged, was on the floor.

I wondered if she'd been out when they fucked her. I wondered if her parents would be so smug about the exorbitant private school fees when this came to light. Her school was one of the best, by which I mean most expensive: that's the only real criterion for that stratum of Australian society.

I heard a thump and a shuffle, feet dragging on what passed for carpet.

I levelled my gat. Trev did likewise beside me, but sufficiently distant so one shotgun blast couldn't hit us both. Old habits.

We greeted druggie arsehole number two as he stumbled into the room, bottle of bourbon in his hand and his limp penis hanging out of his soiled Y-fronts. The only other clothing he was wearing were dirty, mismatched socks. He shuddered to a halt as he tried to take in the gun-metal artillery facing him.

'Sit the fuck down!' I ordered.

'Wha …'

Trev didn't wait for him to finish. He stepped in and pistol-whipped the fucker. Cunty screamed and dropped to his knees. Trev grabbed him by the neck and moved him to the free armchair.

I turned to Tanya. 'Hey, babe, can you please check on her? Make sure she's still alive?'

Tanya moved over to the shagged schoolgirl. 'Yeah, there's a pulse, and she's breathing, although a bit shallow.'

She stepped over to Trev's hostage. 'Who fucked her, arsehole?'

The junkie was having trouble focusing. Even more so after Tanya broke his nose with the butt of her revolver.

'If she was out of it, that's called rape, you fucking piece of shit.'

I stepped in. 'Okay, babe. Enough. We'll get help for her, soon. Right now we need to find the jewels.'

She stepped back. 'Okay, Harry. But I can't fucking stand rapists.'

'I know, babe. Maybe he'll need a bit of pain in a minute, for our purposes, and you can oblige.'

I turned back to idiot boy. 'Okay, arsehole, Natasha told us the jewels are here. Start talking. Now!'

In a flash of true inspirational genius, he looked at me and said, 'Fuck you.'

The next Rhodes Scholar this boy certainly was not. I grabbed a cushion from beside him and held it over his right knee.

'Babe? Barrel against the cushion and one bullet into his kneecap.'

'Oh, yes please.' Tanya brought her five-shot up and pushed it into the cushion. One muffled blast.

Idiot shrieked like a bitch.

I seized his blubbering face by the jaw. 'Are you Dwayne?'

'Yes,' he sniffed.

'Good. Your little slag girlfriend, Natasha, told us you've got some jewels stashed here that don't belong to you.'

'I don't know what you're talking about,' he bawled. 'You can't trust anything Tash says.'

'Okay, we'll do this the hard way.' I pulled my gat back out and put the muzzle against his uninjured knee. 'With one knee fucked, you'll still be walking, only with a limp and a stick for life. With both fucked, you'll be in a wheelchair. Fancy that, do you, arsehole?'

As he was contemplating his next inspired life choice, a vaguely anthropomorphic noise emanated from the other chair. I'm guessing it was on the spectrum of a Neanderthal man being awoken by an intruder in his grotto.

Anyway, Captain Caveman upped the ante, yelling, 'What the fuck?', as he hauled his scrawny body upright, grabbing a blade from somewhere in the armchair.

His problem, well one of the many, was he didn't know who to focus on. Always a hard tactical situation to find oneself in. A truly unfathomable conundrum for a drugged-up retard like this specimen.

Tanya was closest to him, but if the state of the girl on the couch was any indication, both our opiate heroes were rock-solid male chauvinists. And so caveman probably didn't register Tanya as any sort of threat. Bad, bad move, son.

Instead he made a lunge for Trev, who was between me and him. The fact Trev had his .357 levelled at him didn't seem to dent his bravado.

As he lunged, the female threat he'd disregarded came good. Of course she did: Tan never, ever failed to step up to the mark.

One of the many stunning attributes I love about her.

She dropped onto one leg and with the other she swept idiot's feet out from under him. He collapsed on his face like a sack of shit, his rusty fishing knife bouncing away from him. As he scrabbled for it, Trev stomped his heel onto his hand. I heard the crunch of bones breaking.

'Is this what you're after, arsehole?' said Tanya, picking up the weapon.

She leant down and drove it into his groin. He squealed at almost a dog-whistle pitch as the manky blade cut into his junk.

'That's for her over there on the couch. Might put you off sex for a while, not to mention rape,' she said, twisting the knife around in his genitals. Blood spread around his trousers.

'On your feet, cunt,' I said to the dude in front of me. He was transfixed by Tanya neutering his buddy.

I gave him a slap to get his attention. 'Take me to the stash, or lose your other knee.'

'Okay, okay,' he blubbered, hauling himself onto his good leg.

The room out the back was an Aladdin's cave on steroids. Or more likely heroin in this place. Electronic gear (computers, laptops, phones, tablets) was stacked everywhere. Hop-along limped over to a shelf unit and pointed to a wooden box.

'They're in there. Please don't hurt me anymore.'

I shoved him out of the way. He fell over. Occupational hazard of a kneecap with a bullet in it.

The box wasn't locked. The inside gleamed like an overpopulated magpie's nest: a shitload of jewelry.

I rifled through and found all of great-aunt Ethel's bequest. I pocketed them.

'How come you haven't fenced these?' I said as I kicked the dude in the ribs.

He groaned. 'The guy we use, he's in remand until he can make bail.'

The prick obviously had no idea how much the stuff was worth, especially the ruby beetle brooch.

I turned to Trev. 'Let's bring Natasha in and then get the hell out of here.'

'Roger that, brother. I'll just put this one out to it,' said Trev, pulling a syringe from his pocket. He removed the cap and knelt, grabbing the dude's arm. He stuck the needle in and pushed on the plunger.

'What is it?' shrieked idiot.

'You're going to have a good sleep for hours, fuckwit. Good night.'

'What …' was all he could utter before his eyes closed.

'I'll go and do the other one. You guys grab Natasha,' said Trev.

'Actually, I'll do the other guy,' said Tanya. 'Allow me to renew the acquaintance already.' She smirked mischievously.

As I walked out the back door with Trev, I could hear the shrieking from inside the house. I didn't think that dude was ever going to screw another woman in his life. Mind you, hardly any loss to the females of the species.

We pulled the unconscious Natasha out of the van, carried her into the house, and dropped her on the floor next to her sleeping boyfriend, removing her gag and cable ties.

The screaming had stopped and Tanya rejoined us, grinning. 'Girl's got to get job satisfaction, Harry.'

'No argument here. I love to see my staff happy on the job.'

'Be a lot happier when I get the fuck out of here and get a drink,' said Trev.

'Now you're talking,' said Tanya.

'Okay, team, let's hit the road.'

'You drive, Harry,' said Trev. 'I'll make the call.'

As I pulled the van out onto the street, and headed north, Trev used one of his untraceable mobiles to call the cops and report an unconscious rape victim, a gunshot wound, a stabbing victim, and a house full of stolen goods.

As we cruised back along Botany Road towards the city, and our version of civilization, two cop cars and an ambulance, all with lights flashing and sirens blaring, shot past us heading south.

– 5 –

Sylvie sat across my desk from me, tears trickling down her alabaster cheeks as she touched her great-aunt's jewels laid out on my desk blotter.

Trev and Tanya were over on the couch, enjoying a well-earned drink, as was I, of course.

'How will I ever thank you enough?' Sylvie said, gazing wantonly into my eyes. The look said she'd had a taste of the Kenmare lingual prowess and she wanted more.

'We can sort that out. I'm just rapt we got your jewels back. I really thought they would have gone.'

'You're my hero, Harry.' The mien was more than wanton now. A quick glance over to the couch and I saw Tanya's eyes rolling.

Sylvie looked down as she stroked the ruby beetle. It felt strangely delicious to have a piece of jewelry worth at least a quarter of a million sitting on my desk.

There'd never been anything near that valuable in my crappy office before.

Except gorgeous women, and they are beyond valuation.

Sylvie looked back at me. Her tongue rode a nervous little foray across her lips. The ingénue was resurfacing. Still cute.

I was generally averse to having an audience for my carnal pursuits, but I couldn't help picturing myself defiling Sylvie on my desk right now, despite my team in the room.

Still, it wasn't to be.

Tanya came over and put her hand on Sylvie's shoulder. 'Let's go celebrate, girlfriend. Leave these old dudes to do their dude stuff.'

Sylvie beamed at Tanya. I was thinking Tanya was the one who was going to be getting lucky with Sylvie tonight, not me. Ah well, it wasn't as if I'd exactly missed out.

'What about the jewels?' asked Sylvie.

'No problems. They can go in the safe over there,' I said. 'We can sort out a more permanent arrangement in due course.'

'Thank you, my hero.' She leant across the desk and kissed me on the mouth. No lack of tongue. I barred up.

'Okay, boys,' said Tanya. 'I'm taking Sylvie for a girls' celebration drink. See you both tomorrow.'

She winked at me. Cheeky. Fuck, I loved her.

The girls left and Trev grabbed the bottle of Jameson, refilling our glasses. He sat opposite me.

'Well, that was an interesting job, Mr Kenmare. Rather more so than usual.'

'Indeed it was, Mr Matson. No cash, I'm afraid.'

Trev sniggered. 'Yeah, although you got well and truly compensated. Turned pro bono into pro boner.'

I cracked up. That was a good one.

'You'll just have to owe me, Harry. Or get a case with a hunky, gay client.'

'Fair call, we'll work on that. Tanya's done well, mind you. Sylvie said she wants her to have the pearls.'

Trev whistled. 'Nice. But judging by the way the two of them left, I reckon Tanya's in for more than just the pearls tonight.'

'Young lust, absolutely beautiful. The world needs more of it.'

'Cheers to that.'

We chinked glasses.

– 6 –

Two hours later, I opened the door to my apartment. I had in mind a well-deserved bottle of Bordeaux with a tin of French duck terrine and a Romy Schneider movie, from my extensive collection.

I never tire of Romy, one of my all-time favourite actresses. I never tire fantasizing about getting naked with her either. Alas, I'd need a time machine for that, with Romy's sad, premature departure from the planet back in the 80s.

I closed the door behind me, before I noticed the soft, warm glow from my bedroom. After a second, the pungent aroma raped my nostrils. Unmistakeably fresh in my memory: Sylvie's pussy. Then I heard the moaning.

I dumped my keys on the hall-stand and stepped into my play chamber. What the fuck sort of paradise had I walked into?

The bed, my bed, was stripped back to make one big playground. Tanya and Sylvie were naked and gorging themselves in the sexiest sixty-niner I had ever witnessed in my entire, debauched life. And, believe me, I've seen some of the best, usually first-hand.

Tanya, on top, looked up from Sylvie's crotch, her face glistening in the candlelight. She was smothered in Sylvie's juices. She grinned.

'About time, Mr PI. We're on thirds already, so we're overdue for some good, hard cock.'

Sylvie's face, glistening as well, peered around from behind Tanya's thigh. 'Oh, my hero is here, finally. I need to pay my bill, Harry.'

I ripped my clothes off. Bugger Romy and the Bordeaux.

Actually, I would love to bugger Romy, but alas, fantasies …

Back to the job at hand.

The bill was getting paid ten times over now. My biggest dilemma as I removed my last sock and climbed onto the bed, penis upstanding and throbbing for action, was where the hell to put it first?

The girls solved the conundrum.

They pushed me back and jointly sucked my cock for a couple of glorious minutes.

'You want his cock first, or his tongue?' Tanya whispered to Sylvie.

'Oh, god, I want both.'

I watched Tanya tongue-kiss her. Damn, it was sexy.

Tanya slipped her tongue out from Sylvie's lips. 'Girlfriend, you'll be getting both before the night's out. Just a case of how we start.'

Sylvie giggled. 'Okay, I'll take his tongue. I'm an addict already.'

'You and me both, sister.' Tanya kissed her again and swivelled, lowering her sodden pussy onto my rod. Oh, fuck that was good.

Then Sylvie's crotch dulled my vision as it descended onto my face. Her aroma was even stronger than on my last visit. In fact, the last time I'd smelt something this pungent was out the back of the fish market. I clutched her buttocks and plunged my wicked tongue into her pussy.

I'm an atheist. But I'd found heaven.

* * *

– Case #5 –

WANKERS

She had a Sunday school face with a body that said Saturday night. She slinked toward me in sling-back heels like I was prey.

- Frank De Blase

WANKERS

– 1 –

She had a rack that would've distracted a Catholic priest from the altar boys. My first client in a fortnight sashayed unannounced into my shitty, smoke-filled office as I was pouring my first Jameson for the day. Well, it was a touch after 11 a.m. I nearly spilt the amber nectar. I was transfixed. She reached my desk and held out her hand.

'Carmen Garcia.'

I took her hand. Firm grip. I liked that in a woman. It spoke volumes.

'Harry Kenmare, Private Investigator, at your service.'

'Good.' The siren's smile, combined with her rack, must have destroyed dozens of poor rogues over the years.

I smiled back and thought to myself she wasn't calmin' anything. Quite the opposite in fact. But I kept that lame line to myself.

Carmen sat down and opened her blue Gucci handbag. Matched her magnetic eyes, but I guess she'd worked it that way. She pulled out a cigarette case and lit up. Then she extracted two envelopes: one slim, the other chunkier.

I like chunky envelopes almost as much as melonious breasts.

I was alternating my eyes between them, and the envelopes.

'Look at me, shamus. Perhaps you can play with these puppies later.' She heaved her chest out dramatically to make the point. Two actually. 'You've got some work to do first.'

'Of course. You have my undivided attention, Carmen.'

She slid a photo across to me from the fat envelope. I could see the delicious, filthy lucre stacked in there.

'My daughter, Solara.'

'Runaway?'

'Yes. Family misunderstandings. I won't bore you. But I want you to find her.'

'Bring her home?' I had to ask, but I always hated those runaway jobs where retrieval was the object. A middle-aged, male PI trying to persuade a young woman into a vehicle looked more sinister than it was. It risked unwanted intervention.

'No,' she said.

That surprised me.

'No, I'd like her home, but it has to be her choice. She's an adult, just.'

Bugger me. Progressive parent. Unusual.

'Cool. So, what do you want me to do?'

She slid the slimmer envelope towards me.

'Find her. Then give her this and ask her to read it. That's all you have to do.'

I picked it up. It was sealed.

'Any leads?' I asked.

'Her best friend confided that she's doing naked dancing.'

Most mothers I'd met would be staring into their laps at this point, but not Carmen. I suspected she'd had a bit of exotic work experience herself.

'Pole dancing?' I asked.

'No. Apparently some place where you dance in a room on your own. Sounds a bit strange to me.'

Ah, yes. I decided not to get descriptive.

'I know the places. Strip shows without a pole.' I could be the master of understatement when required.

'I'll take your word for it,' she murmured.

She pushed the fat envelope over. I tried not to be too speedy in grabbing Big Boy.

'Five grand up front for expenses,' she said. 'When the job is done, there'll be another five waiting for you.'

Yeah, I'd figured she waltzed in from the rich end of town.

For them, money is no object when they want something. And they buy people the way they buy things. Capitalism, left unchecked: sordid and mercenary. But business is business. I'm sure as hell not going to be changing society.

'So, I just rock up and give Solara this, and report back?'

The alluring grin again. I was hooked.

'Almost. But you must take a photo of Solara holding the envelope and send it to me. Then you come see me. Deal?'

'Deal.' I stood up, held my hand across the desk, and we shook.

As she was still holding it, she smirked at me and ran her tongue along her bright-cerise lips.

'And when you visit to collect your payment, there could be certain non-cash bonuses. I like detectives.'

I wanted to fuck her on my desk right now. But this lady knew her priorities, so even my deepest Kenmare charm would've been futile. I'd have to show some penile patience.

'I'll look forward to that, Carmen. You're a very beautiful lady.'

I always thought a compliment went down well, so it was obligatory behaviour in my books.

Of course, in this era of slavish political correctness, I have come a gutser on occasion: been rebuked, and even slapped. What the fuck sort of world have we landed in where a bloke can't tell a woman she's beautiful?

Carmen smirked saucily. 'I'll take the compliment, Harry, but lose the "lady" description.'

She winked, blew me a kiss, and left my office.

My erection and I stood in stunned silence.

– 2 –

The following afternoon, I started with the wank-tanks: what polite society referred to, in hushed tones, as peep shows. The street name is more accurate. I knew four main ones. The first three yielded nothing.

Now, there's no such thing as an up-market wank-tank, but there are degrees of grubbiness.

And I left the least grubby until last.

I descended the dimly lit stairs to Voyeurs & Vixens. I pressed the buzzer and waved at the camera. The secure door wasn't there to try and keep anyone out as such, since these businesses wanted all the visiting desperados they could get. It was simply a delaying mechanism for the occasions the coppers turned up. The rules dictated the shows could only have one girl performing alone: live sex was not allowed. Of course, girl-on-girl action was where the revenue lay. Hence the door delay meant a warning light could be flashed in the performance chamber and one girl could scamper out the back door, leaving one worked up tart to play with herself. And so one wildly masturbating lady is what the coppers always got to see. Only they didn't have to pay.

The door clicked and I stepped into the dingy cavern beyond. I walked over to the customer counter. Gazza, the manager, and a regular information source and sometime drinking buddy of mine, was sitting behind it. I also occasionally slung him some work doing static surveillance for me. Helped me out in busy times and helped him pay his rent and booze bills.

Gazza, formerly Sergeant Garry Dawes of the Australian Commando Regiment, was a minus a leg, several metres of intestines, and half his face. His disability and disfigurement didn't lead to massive employment options. He'd found out the hard way the words from the Traveling Wilburys song about no one giving a damn were bang on the money. In his case, the Australian government didn't give a rat's arse about him leaving his body parts by a roadside in Afghanistan. Especially since he opened his mouth about the fourteen dead schoolchildren who some scrotum in intel had determined were Taliban fighters hiding out. They'd locked him in a psych hospital when he came home, which probably fucked him up more than the Afghan arseholes. But with his habit of posting virulent, anarchic rants on the Internet, the government still hated him. Or so he told me repeatedly.

So now, his compo cut off, Gazza had to scrape a living in here. His twelve-hour shifts consisted of encouraging the girls to do as much dildo work as possible, and preferably anal (great for business). Then it was cleaning the booths every few hours: bucket-loads of sodden tissues, and cum deposits on the walls from the lazy fucks who didn't bother with the Kleenex.

Yeah, Gazza was simply drowning in the gratitude of his country. So whenever I could, I gave him some work.

'How's it hanging, Gazza?'

'Badly to the left, Harry. The old Afghan gait.'

We both laughed. We did every time, never tiring of the joke.

'Should have a bit of surveillance work in the next couple of weeks, mate.'

'That'd be much appreciated, brother. Cleaning up after these fuckstains barely covers the rent, let alone getting on the piss. The only upside are the girls.'

I pulled out the photo of Solara, along with five hundred of my expenses money: figured no informant deserved it more than Gazza. I slid the folded bundle across his counter, along with the photo.

'Jeez, you're exceptionally generous today, Harry. Thanks, mate.'

'Least I can do, brother.' I tapped the photo.

'Yeah, absolutely,' he said without blinking. 'I wouldn't forget her face, or those tits, or the arse. She's fucking smoking hot, that one.'

'Working here then?'

He laughed. 'Of course, mate. After the butt-naked audition, I had to hire her. Started last week. She'll be on in a couple of hours.'

'Sweet. Unusual glint in those eyes, Gazza?'

'Yeah. She's one of those sympathy skanks. Blew me. It was great.'

'Good on ya, mate.'

Gazza's 'sympathy skanks' were the girls who listened to him about Afghanistan (how the Taliban had fucked up his sex life, along with everything else) and felt sorry enough for him to put out.

I looked back at the photo of Solara and tried to picture her sucking my dick. Yep, that image worked. Mind you, so did that of her mother, and Carmen was a red-hot prospect.

I waved in the direction of the tanks.

'What's the talent like in there at the moment?'

'Pretty bloody good actually. Two Dutch backpackers. And what they won't do to each other isn't even in the sealed section of the Kama Sutra.'

'Yeah? Dutch, I've always thought they're a pretty liberated lot.'

He smirked. 'Take a look, mate. Expand your definition of "liberated". Those two will rip open the windmills of your mind.'

He gave me a bag of two-dollar coins.

I went into the nearest available booth, trying to breathe through my mouth to reduce the cloying smell of semen, fresh and stale. I put a small stack of coins on the shelf next to the window, ready to feed the machine. First coin into the slot and the shutter in the viewing panel clicked open. I peered through the glass.

Gazza wasn't wrong. Tulip and Daffodil, or whatever they were called, were eating each other out with more enthusiasm than a busload of refugees in a McDonald's. Judging by the toys and lube tubes laid out on the mattress next to them, the best was yet to come.

Another coin.

The voice in the tank to my left was pure primate, grunting like a rutting gorilla.

The music increased in tempo, and so did the pride of Holland. Tulip, without slowing her pussy munching, greased a dildo the size of my forearm and eased it into Daffodil's arsehole, driving it in at least twenty centimetres.

Another coin.

Daffodil's ecstatic howling at the anal intrusion was clearly a motivation for the ape next door who finally bellowed some humanoid language.

'You dirty fucking sluts, I fucking love you!'

Slap, slap, slap, slap, slap, GRUNT!

Who was it who said something about a hundred chimpanzees left alone with typewriters would eventually produce Shakespeare? Yeah, not sure, but monkey-man next door wouldn't be much help to them.

Still, the busty Dutch delights had been worth a look, they did have some talent.

Another coin, or ten. No point wasting the opportunity to enjoy some more girl-on-girl. After the anal adventures, they went face to face riding a double-ender, licking each other's juices off their mouths. Outstanding. I'm not sure this was what the Australian Border Force, or 'Border Farce' as we knew it locally, had in mind when they'd issued the girls' work visas. But I reckon they were far better suited to this line of work than they would be to their visa-designated fruit picking and farmwork.

I silently bade them farewell, thanked Gazza, and headed out into the sultry, darkening evening to kill some time at a bar.

– 3 –

Two hours later, Gazza had introduced me to Solara and I was sitting in the changing room with her. She was topless, and divine.

'Your mother sent me. She said there'd been some family misunderstanding. Guess her peace offering is in this envelope.'

Solara snorted. 'Bitch.'

'So, what was the misunderstanding?' I asked, trying not to fixate on her full, pert breasts.

'Mum brings her new boyfriend home. He touches me up and suggests I join him and mum for a threesome. I don't call that a fucking misunderstanding.'

'See your point.'

Mind you, I could see the boyfriend's point as well: this was a mother-daughter combo to have wet dreams about.

'Yeah, so did he, the sick fuck. I kneed him so hard in his nuts he was on the floor for ten minutes. Mum tried to talk me around. I told her to go fuck herself and packed my bag.'

'Fair enough. Well, she said to give you this and it would explain things. And I've got to get a photo of you with the envelope.'

She frowned at me.

'So I can prove I've done the job. I need to get paid, young lady.'

She smiled. 'Okay. Give me your phone and sit forward a bit. Hold the envelope.'

She manoeuvred behind me, her breasts perched on my right shoulder. With one hand she held my phone in front of us, and with the other she turned my head so the side of my face was pressed into her bosom.

'Hold it up, Harry.'

'It's up all right, babe.' I held the envelope under my chin. Flash.

We looked at the salacious selfie. I couldn't help laughing. It was a shot for my album all right. And she wore a wicked smile that said, 'Fuck you, Mum.'

She gave me the phone back. I texted the photo to Carmen.

– 4 –

I woke late the next morning. After meeting Solara, I'd lubricated my fantasies generously at the Emerald Bar.

I was getting dressed when the phone rang. I answered.

'G'day, Gazza. Everything okay?'

'Don't know, Harry. A couple of suss-looking guys been snooping around the front and back.'

'Mate, you run a wank-tank. You attract suss guys like flies to shit.'

'These two are different. I'm getting a vibe, Harry. Reckon they might be government, coming for me.'

'Gazza, I'm sure the fucking government, as much as they are total wankers, have really lost interest in you by now.'

'Not that simple. Couple of things I haven't told you, mate. Can you drop in? Like soon?'

'Yeah, of course, mate. See you shortly.'

'Thanks, Harry.' He rang off.

I was inclined to put it down to Gazza's never-ending, although understandable, paranoia. His mind had become a quagmire of conspiracy theories. But he was a mate, and he'd asked for help.

And true mates always answer the call.

I got on my way to Voyeurs & Vixens.

I pressed the buzzer at the front door, but to no avail, twice. Strange. I couldn't see anyone in the vicinity. It was possible Gazza had gone for a crap, if there were no customers.

I pulled out my phone and called him. It went to voicemail. Okay, that was more than strange. That was a warning sign. Gazza always had his phone, even in the crapper. I knew it from awful experience: I couldn't ever forget the call that sounded like boulders being dropped down a well.

I legged it around the block to the back entrance in the laneway. The normally locked door was resting on its latch. I wished I'd packed my .38 Special. I had an ominous feeling about this. And my old gut instinct was seldom wrong.

Not that I've always listened carefully: my personal life bears painful testament to my inattention.

I slipped inside silently. I could hear Gazza's articulate defiance: 'Fuck you, cunts!'

Another male voice: 'We'll see about that, arsehole.'

A loud smack of flesh on flesh. Then another.

I moved down the short corridor and found one of Gazza's girls, stark naked, hiding in the doorway to the performance chamber.

I leant in to whisper in her ear, trying not to get distracted by her delightful body.

'I'm Harry, a friend of Gazza.'

'Lissa,' she sighed in my ear. She smelt floral, and edible.

'How many of them?'

'Two that I saw.'

'Know who they are?'

'No. Never seen them before. But they've been hurting him.'

'See if you can find anything to use as a weapon and then follow me.'

'Like what?'

'Something you can do some damage with.'

I moved stealthily forward. I saw Gazza in his wheelchair, blood running out of his nose and with cut lips. Two goons were standing over him.

I strode in fast.

'Takes a real brave cunt to hit a disabled bloke, especially with two of you. You fucking weak pricks!' I kept the forward momentum, readying my fists.

The pair of thugs turned. The one closest didn't have time to react before my fist slammed into his gut, right in the solar plexus. He doubled over and hit the floor.

I needed to take out the other one, but he was now ready for me. He blocked my first swipe and returned the favour, his fist smacking into my jaw. That hurt. I went in to wrestle him. Over his shoulder I saw Gazza move on his wheels, a large hunting knife in his right hand. Whilst walking wasn't exactly Gazza's forte these days, there was nothing wrong with his arms, well muscled from doing more than their fair share. He drove the shiny steel blade square into the goon's arsehole. He shrieked and collapsed on his knees. I drove my fist into his throat and he keeled over.

'Behind ya!' yelled Gazza.

I spun and lowered myself as the other thug came at me. I needn't have worried. He never made it.

Lissa's breasts moved magnificently through the air as she swung a fire extinguisher full force into the goon's head. The clunking sound was sickening. He dropped like a sack of shit and didn't move again.

The goon with the lacerated rectum was moaning on the floor. I grabbed his hair and belted his head into the edge of the counter until he passed out.

'You okay, Gazza?'

'Bit of claret, Harry, that's all. But they were only just warming up, so bloody glad you turned up. And, Lissa, thank you, honey.'

'No worries, Gazza.'

'Yeah, top work, babe,' I added. 'Tough and sexy. Great combination.'

She beamed at me. 'Well, handsome, any time you're into paying, then I'm into playing.'

'I'll keep that in mind.'

She headed back to the girls' changing room.

'So, who are these fuckers, Gazza, and what did they want with you?'

'They didn't exactly introduce themselves, mate, but they'll be government arseholes. Wanted to impress upon me the need to keep my mouth shut.'

'Why now?'

'I put out a few new blogs last week. Obviously upset the good folks down in Canberra.'

'Mate, you need to be more careful.'

'I'm a bit past that stage, Harry. Here, take this.'

He pulled out a small, cloth bag from under his counter and handed it to me.

'Mate, it's a hard drive with a whole lot of shit on it. Enough to destroy careers and maybe even bring down the government.'

'What do you want me to do with it?'

'It's only a matter of time, Harry. Something will happen to me, I'm in their sights. There's instructions in there. Promise me, please, mate.'

'Yeah, of course. But let's hope that won't be necessary.'

'It will, mate. Now we better sort out these fuckers.'

I went through their pockets. No wallets, phones, or anything identifying. One of them had a set of picklocks. I pocketed them. And they explained the back door.

'Nothing on them at all means spooks,' said Gazza.

'Or thugs hired by the spooks. Either way, government.'

'Any ideas? We can't exactly call the cops.'

I let my devious mind run wild.

'No, not as such, but thinking outside the square, yes we can. You got a small freezer bag and sugar?'

He frowned. 'Yeah, in the kitchen back there.'

I returned a minute later with a plastic snap-lock bag full of white sugar. I shoved it in one of the goon's inside jacket pockets.

'Gazza, your camera out back's the only one out there?'

'Yeah, no others.'

'Does it record anywhere?'

'No, mate. Just for watching on the monitor here.'

'Cool.'

I dragged both inert thugs out into the quiet back lane. I got Gazza's knife, wiped his prints off it, and took it outside. I wrapped the hand of the goon with the intact arsehole around the knife handle. I closed and locked the door behind me as I returned inside.

'Now call it in, Gazza. You saw two guys fighting in the lane with a bag of white powder and a large knife. That'll motivate the local constabulary.' I winked at him.

He grinned. 'You're a class act, Harry.'

In less than two minutes, we watched on screen as three patrol units screeched into the lane. The cops tumbled out of their cars with guns drawn. The two goons, now semi-conscious, were dragged away.

On my way out, I got Lissa's phone number.

– 5 –

I called Gazza the next morning to check he was okay. The conspiracy theories had come to visit early today: he was convinced more government enforcers would be on their way for him. I wondered what was on that hard drive. Was it something earth-shattering or was it a confection of Gazza's fucked-up realities? I'd read the instructions: details about loading it onto the Web if Gazza disappeared or died. More paranoia, no doubt. But then, those hoods yesterday were the real deal. I grinned as I imagined the pair of them doubtless still trying to convince the cops they weren't brawling drug-dealers.

Gazza said he was off to a public rally this afternoon. The Defence Minister and the Minister for Veterans' Affairs were making a public address about the issues facing returning vets, in particular the spiralling suicide rate that was finally getting some traction in the media.

And not before bloody time: our service personnel deserved a much better deal.

'Gazza, that's sure to be a complete pile of insincere garbage. Why are you bothering?'

'Mate, I want to give those fuckers a piece of my mind. Bit of good old-fashioned, town-square heckling.'

'Fair enough, have fun.'

'Oh, I will, Harry. You've no idea. As a great man said, "Let your plans be dark as night and when you move, fall like a thunderbolt".'

'Sun Tzu, if my memory serves.'

'Spot on. Anyway, mate, thanks for everything.'

'No worries, catch you soon.'

'Yeah. See ya, Harry.' He hung up.

My gut feeling twitched. Badly.

– 6 –

After lunch I flicked on the TV in my office to the twenty-four-hour news channel. After a few headlines they crossed live to the veterans' rally. The two ministers were standing on a small platform taking it in turns to melt the microphones with the hot air of their patronizing pontifications.

Fuck, I hate the political class.

The camera angle changed to show more of the crowd, who were raucous in jeering the politicians.

I saw Gazza in his wheelchair. Given his infirmities, other vets had given him space at the front of the crowd, along with two other chair-bound men. Gazza's wheelchair had a folded beach umbrella attached to its side, looking like a flagpole. That seemed a bit odd, given there was no rain forecast. And since Gazza was sitting in the blazing sunshine, he clearly wasn't interested in it as a parasol either.

Gazza was getting right into the heckling, and if the frequency of the word 'wankers' being shouted by him was anything to go by, the pair on stage must have been the record holders for ministerial masturbation.

Finally, the question time started, and Gazza was on the front foot, so to speak, asking the ministers why his compo had been cut off. The politicians clearly knew his case, as they both gave banal answers using his name.

But that was as far as question time got.

I watched, stunned, as Gazza reached into the folds of his beach umbrella and pulled out an M16. He wasted no time. Butt to his shoulder, two quick bursts of automatic fire left both ministers dying on the stage.

My mouth was still hanging open as Gazza turned the rifle, swallowed the muzzle, and pulled the trigger one last time. The top of his head exploded off in a shower of blood.

– 7 –

I swallowed two stiff drinks and sat in melancholic, smoky silence at my desk.

What a fucked-up world.

Even if I'd been trying, I couldn't have felt any sympathy for the dead politicians.

Not because I'm an anarchist, I'm not. Well, maybe a little: those Irish genes. No, rather because the reason decent people like Gazza get sent to warzones that have nothing to do with us, and have their lives fucked over, is because of decisions made by politicians. A bunch of self-serving, egotistical wankers who are interested in power and privilege, and who are happy to fuck Joe Citizen up the arse.

I read Gazza's notes again and got on the phone to my offsider, Trev. He did all my techie stuff.

He arrived forty minutes later and fiddled on his laptop with Gazza's hard drive plugged into it.

'It's not that hard, Harry, you fucking Luddite. You gotta get with the age, brother.'

'Mate, I'm from a different age. And I've got my skills.'

'Your predominant talents, aside from being a good detective occasionally, are drinking and fucking.'

'And the problem is?'

'Just saying.'

'Mate, the only problem is there's no Olympic event for either. If there was, in this sport-obsessed country I'd be a fucking national hero.'

Trev chortled.

We watched in silence the surreptitious footage from Afghanistan: an Australian commander giving the orders, some of the soldiers hesitating, soldiers being yelled at and threatened, being called cowards.

Then the brutal barrage of fire-power.

All the bloodied bodies of the school kids and their teacher.

The panicked orders from the officers starting the official cover-up.

And on went Gazza's pseudo-documentary with secretly recorded conversations and copies of documents. It sure was career-ending stuff for a whole lot of people in the Establishment.

'Fuck them,' I said. 'Trev, do it, mate.'

'Roger that. Hold on to your seats, folks. This is going to be massive.'

Trev had tried explaining to me about offshore proxy servers and untraceable IP addresses and a whole lot of boring shit I couldn't follow. I was only interested in results.

And we got them all right.

In less than half an hour, the impact was hitting, with the unsourced material erupting forth. The Internet and the media went into meltdown, and the Australian government was following fast.

Me? I needed to find solace in the raw sordidness of sex.

Nothing can compare in reminding you of your humanity. No philosophical musing comes close to sex for answering those existential questions.

I made a phone call.

– **8** –

A large terrace house in a leafy Paddington street was Carmen's well-heeled residence.

I hefted the brass knocker, armed with a cold bottle of Veuve.

She opened the door. She was wearing a translucent, cobalt-blue negligée.

She pulled me through the doorway, slamming it closed.

'So, detective, time to investigate my body.'

'Madam, rest assured it will be a seriously thorough investigation. And a very long and hard one.'

'Just how I like it.'

She plunged her tongue into my mouth with more vigour than a Viking entering an English convent.

Time to pillage and plunder, I reckoned.

She rushed me upstairs and we got naked at warp speed.

Carmen gave head like an angel, of the fallen variety.

By the time I had assuaged my desperate base desires an hour later, she'd fallen a lot further.

She lay asleep next to me.

Some semblance of calm returned to my mind.

Gazza, rest in peace, brother. You had the last word on those wankers.

*   *   *

– Case #6 –

THE MISSING LILY

She was the kind of girl that older dentists find attractive. She had a nice set of teeth, a fair set of knockers, and a lousy set of values.

- Kinky Friedman

THE MISSING LILY

– 1 –

Panda bear, pick-up, pussy, phone call, pagodas, Peking duck, paternal loss, prostitutes, pay-day, and pussy galore.

So, the question is: what do these ten Ps have in common?

And the answer is: the most recent assignment for me, PI Harry Kenmare.

Being a gumshoe sure as hell has variety. Just as well. If I had to do the nine-to-five corporate hamster wheel ever again, I'd fucking shoot myself.

I was enjoying a post-dinner cigar in the beer garden of my favourite watering hole, the Emerald Bar, along with a large Jameson on ice, part of my staple diet. Sydney's summer was lingering late this year. So despite being April, the stifling, evening humidity left me sweatier than a Bangkok streetwalker's crotch. At least I smelt better.

I'd had enough of the rivulets of perspiration running down my back, so I extinguished my Cuban, sliding the unsmoked half back into its metal tube for a future blissful puff. I downed my whiskey and headed for the air-conditioned interior.

The waitress who served my dinner, Tia, was out of her uniform and sitting at the bar. A giant panda bear was perched on the stool to her left.

Tia and I always flirted. Nothing had ever happened, only verbal fun. Mind you, at twenty years my junior, with a gorgeous brown-eyed face, long blonde hair, enticing pert breasts, and a svelte body to drool over, I wouldn't have said 'no' to more. But I'd seen her friendly with other punters, so I figured that was simply her gregarious nature and even my Kenmare charm wouldn't stand a chance. Plus, being my local pub, I wasn't going to rock the boat with unwelcome advances on the staff, no matter how alluring they were.

The old adage has some merit: don't shit where you eat.

I got myself a fresh Jameson and planted my arse on the stool to Tia's right.

'Hey, Harry.'

'Nice panda.'

She sniggered. 'Well, that beats the line about etchings. And I thought you were admiring my tits.'

I grinned at her. 'I was, but I reckoned it'd be more polite to compliment your panda. You know, political correctness and all that shit.'

'Shit indeed.' She rolled her eyes. 'Mr Panda here is a present for my niece. It's her seventh birthday tomorrow.'

I tried not to think of my own daughter. Little Orla, nine years old, and never saw her tenth birthday. Abducted, raped and murdered years ago. Fifteen years.

Some days it feels as raw as fifteen hours.

I refocused on my drink and fantasized about sex with Tia.

Drink and sex usually allay my demons. Not exactly my doctor's advice, but you get that.

'She'll love it,' I said. 'Now, for the record, I don't think your tits need any compliments, they speak magnificently for themselves.'

'Harry, a girl *always* likes compliments. And I don't give a rat's arse about correctness. Bullshit for the bitter and twisted feminist brigade.'

'I'm with you, Tia.' I winked at her. 'Okay, so can I get on my knees and worship your gorgeous body?'

She giggled. 'Not in here, the boss doesn't like us getting *too* friendly. Even with regulars like you.'

'Well, I've got an altar back at my place, and it's overdue for worship practice.' It was a bit lame, but I sniffed opportunity, of the welcome variety.

She grinned mischievously, glanced at the other staff to make sure no one was looking, and touched my hand. 'Is that the altar you use to sacrifice virgins?'

'Bloody hell. It's been donkey's years since I encountered a virgin. And I think she might have been lying.'

I took a swig of Jameson.

'Do they still exist, virgins?' I grinned.

'No idea. Wouldn't mind seeing the altar, though,' she said, dropping her voice.

'Let's go, then. And I've no use for virgins anymore, my teaching days were over years ago.'

She ran her tongue across her lips. 'Well, Mr Retired Teacher, I need detention, because I'm a very naughty girl.'

I was getting a hard-on.

We left the pub separately. I waited down the street for her and Mr Panda.

Back at my place, it was a race to get naked. She took the gold medal, but only because she didn't have to contest with socks.

A man can't fuck with socks on, at least not if he possesses any self-respect.

She did as she was told and sat on my face: it was a standard command I issued to every woman in my bed. Tia rode my voracious tongue until she screamed in ecstasy. Her thighs clamping orgasmically nearly fractured my bloody jaw. I loved it. Then she wanted to be tied up because she was '*so, so* naughty' and she needed 'to be punished'. Why would I argue? I used four neckties to secure her until she looked like a starfish ready to mate.

'Anything you don't do?'

I never presume.

'Nothing I've ever heard of, so hurry up and fuck me.'

I buried my rock-hard member in her saturated pussy and went hard until I exploded.

Ten minutes later, I untied her, despite her protests and demands to ravish her again.

'Patience, young lady.' I flipped her over and retied her, now a facedown starfish.

'Now, exactly how naughty have you been, Tia?' I whispered in her ear.

'Really fucking wicked, Sir! I need spanking and fucking.'

I slapped her beautiful arse several times. Then I lubed up and slowly slid into her chocolate tunnel. The pillow muffled her howling. Mr Panda sat on the chest of drawers watching the whole show. Panda the pervert.

In the morning, we did two more rounds for good measure. Afterwards, I made her coffee and toast, and she showered. Her and Mr Panda departed. She said she'd be back. I said she could bring a friend. She smirked, told me to get some Viagra, and walked off down the corridor, with an awkward gait that hadn't been there yesterday.

I figure a woman with an awkward gait and a broad smile is one satisfied lady. Well, perhaps not so much of a lady, but you know what I mean.

I smiled to myself and went back inside.

I poured another coffee and was sitting down to relax when the phone rang. The call was being directed through from my office voicemail.

A PI never knocks back potential business.

I pressed 'Accept'.

'Kenmare and Associates. Harry Kenmare speaking.'

A strong Asian accent. 'Mr Kenmare, are you available for work? Good money for you, but urgent job.'

'Yes, I am.'

'Good. Be at Chinese Gardens in one hour. Bench under pagoda next to willow trees. I wear red tie and black suit.'

The line went dead.

– **2** –

Ipaid my entry fee and stepped from bustling Darling Harbour into the serenity and splendour of the magnificent, walled Chinese Gardens. Calling this an oasis from the urban jungle was akin to calling Scarlett Johansson pretty. Of course, if I were wandering these gardens with Scarlett …

Back to reality. I navigated my way along the shady paths next to the impressive water features. My Asian friend wasn't on the first bench that met the description, or the second. There were a hell of a lot of pagodas and willows in this place. But as I came around a bend and saw the third such bench, I saw a lithe, fit Chinese dude in an expensive, slim-cut suit sitting there looking at a folded newspaper.

As I approached, he looked up, revealing a red tie. And the suit was Armani. Nice indeed. Wouldn't mind one myself, but if I had that sort of spare cash, then the sirens of the brothel would call my name.

I sat on the bench keeping a good half-metre between myself and Jackie Chan. I looked at the water lilies in the pond in front of us and waited for my friend to say something.

'You on time, Mr Kenmare. That is good.'

'I'm always on time, my friend. And it's Harry.'

'No need for names. You want the job?'

'I need to know what's involved.'

'All you need to know is twenty thousand dollars for a few hours.'

This guy had to be taking the piss. No one paid that. Unless it was seriously heavy shit and, given where we were in the city, probably triad shit.

'Mate, I need more information. At least tell me who the job is for.'

He stayed silent, as if he were mulling it over, but I knew these inscrutable Orientals. Everything, every detail, would have been pre-planned. This was merely theatre.

'It is twenty thousand and you work for Mr Huang.'

I swallowed. If it was *the* Mr Huang, even 'triad' was an inadequate description. I had to ask.

'You mean Mr Huang, also known as Mr Chinatown?'

'He not like that name. Do not use it. Now, answer my question. You have five seconds to decide.'

Brain said, 'Something is wrong here.' An expensive lifestyle, often beyond my means, yelled, 'Do it!'

I heard my voice say, 'Yes.'

'Good. You know restaurant Five Dragons?'

'Yep.' It was one of the best joints in the heart of Chinatown.

'You go there now. Go upstairs to man at desk. You tell him this: "I have purple orchid from Macau". Repeat it.'

'I have a purple orchid from Macau.'

He stood up. 'Goodbye, Mr Kenmare.'

'Bye, mate.'

He wandered off briskly.

I looked at the water. An enormous, red and black koi carp was mouthing on the surface looking at me. I'm not a lip reader, especially of fish, but I'm sure Mr Carp was saying, 'You stupid fucker.'

Maybe he was right.

– 3 –

At the top of the designated staircase from the restaurant foyer, I was ushered into a small room. Two guys in matching, charcoal-grey Hugo Boss suits looked at me. Like the dude by the pond, their bodies looked incredibly fit, and dangerous. Those almond-shaped, brown eyes looked positively lethal. One of them indicated to me to raise my arms. I assumed the position and had the most thorough body frisk of my life. Had the goon been female, I would have volunteered for a cavity search.

They escorted me through a sliding panel in the wall. The room the other side was enormous and plush, and a bizarre mixture of office and dining-room.

And there was the man.

Mr H was as well toned as his guards, but twenty years older. He didn't smile. His eyes oozed a brutal arrogance.

I guessed Mr H did a lot of business over food, looking at the array of dishes in front of him. A waiter in a white tunic stood off to his side.

The mean bastard on my right pointed to me and then to the chair opposite the big man.

Mr H held up a finger. He finished chewing his mouthful and swallowed. The man had good manners.

I hate people talking through their food.

'Welcome, Mr Kenmare.'

'Mr Huang.' I clearly wasn't getting a handshake, so I nodded my head in deference as I sat down. The slightest movement of the lines by his eyes told me he was satisfied I knew my place.

'You like Peking duck?'

'Absolutely. One of the world's finest dishes.'

'Good.' He said something to the waiter.

Before I could say 'soy sauce', a plate appeared in front of me and was rapidly loaded with duck, rice and bok choy. A large, cold Tsingtao beer was poured.

'Please, enjoy.' Mr H resumed his chewing, so I got stuck in. The duck was to die for.

Food done, fresh beer served, Mr H got down to it.

'Mr Kenmare, my daughter, Lily, is missing. Kidnapped by a rival triad. I need your help.'

I was impressed by his ease in saying 'triad': one of those facts everyone knew, but didn't mention out loud. He must have read my mind.

'I've done my research, Mr Kenmare. Apart from your lady addiction, you have a reputation for efficiency and discretion: two qualities I require above all else. And I know about your daughter, so you understand paternal loss.'

Fuck, this guy was sharp. I'd hate to cross him.

144

'And I'm sorry for your little girl, Mr Kenmare. As the saying goes, "For a father growing old, nothing is dearer than a daughter".'

'Thank you, Mr Huang. And for the Euripides, from memory, I do like the classics.'

I paused to swallow some beer, and spend a second with Orla.

Back to business. 'But if you know who kidnapped Lily, why not get the cops to deal with it?'

There was a hint of a grin. 'Let me show you something.'

He gestured me to follow him to a large screen mounted in the wall. He pressed a switch. The vision was of a circular dining-table with eight men seated around it.

'My most private dining-room. Look closely, please.'

I peered at the image.

Mr H pointed out the two Chinese men. 'My best business managers.' He waved casually at the six Caucasians. 'And I believe you may recognize the others.'

Fuck me, did I ever. Two of the most senior officers from Border Force (or Border Farce as it was known in law enforcement circles), two from the Federal Police, and one who I thought was a Federal Senator. The last white face I didn't know.

'And they're all eating downstairs now?'

'Yes, business.'

'Okay, I recognize the ones from Border Force and the Feds. This one's a Senator, isn't he?'

'Yes. Chairman of the Select Committee on Organized Crime.'

Nice touch, Mr H.

'And this one?' I asked.

'Ah, yes. Not so public. Top boss of the Port Botany Company.'

An importation business being discussed, clearly. With the collection around the table, I had little doubt as to what.

'Keep watching.'

A waiter in a scarlet tunic appeared, pushing a trolley with a large, covered silver platter on it. The lid came off, revealing six fat, brown-paper parcels. They were handed out to the six white men as the trolley slithered its corrupt way around the table.

Mr H smiled at me finally. 'So, Mr Kenmare, our only interest in the police is what they can do for our business. When we have a crime problem, we solve it ourselves. What you see around that table means the unchecked flow of my containers into Port Botany. Those men down there make sure of it, and they are all wealthy as a result. I bring in a hundred kilos of heroin every week. And I am untouchable.'

'Except by your opposition.'

'Very astute, Mr Kenmare. Plus, my Beijing connections ensure the Australian government puts their trade concerns well above thinking about looking too closely at me.'

I thought of youngsters dying on needles full of street-grade drugs, how prohibition was bullshit, the flood of corruption it created, and how it simply meant the rich got richer.

Yeah, my view wasn't going to change shit. I focused back on the here and now.

'Your man said it was twenty thousand?'

'Yes, for about two hours work. But dangerous work.'

Yeah, twenty large would keep me in whiskey and whores for a good while. No qualms. Plus I didn't fancy the idea of saying 'no' to Mr H. I'm sure men had suffered for less.

'I'm all yours, Mr Huang.'

'Excellent decision, Mr Kenmare.'

Yeah, not much choice. The man knew my lifestyle and therefore my price. And, more significantly, he knew my vulnerable spot: missing daughters.

'So, what exactly is the assignment?'

'Lily is being held in a brothel in Hurstville. Triad controlled. Several armed men on the ground floor. We need you to get an appointment with Lily, although they will use a different name for her.'

He handed me a photo. Pretty girl. Would happily see her naked.

He continued, 'You get upstairs with her, where the bedrooms are. Then you open a window so my men can get in silently without a fight. Lily could get hurt if this is not done carefully. There is a back lane that the bedroom windows face on to. But you will need to deal with any window locks.'

'No problems there, those locks are easy. But why not have one of your men go in for an appointment with her? Why me?'

'Because this brothel specializes in Chinese girls for only Western men.'

'And what about dealing with her kidnappers?'

'Not your concern.'

'Okay. You seem to know a lot of detail about the brothel layout.'

He radiated that inscrutable Oriental grin: a charade of charm with an undercurrent of menace and dripping with deviousness. 'Someone at the local council was happy to share the latest building plans with us for a little bonus pay.'

That'd be bloody right. Mind you, looking at the federal law enforcers downstairs and the cash they were getting, a council planning officer would be nothing.

The job was set for tonight.

– 4 –

I got to the brothel, the Canton Concubine, a touch after six. There were no other punters in the lounge and several Asian girls were sitting around indolently. There was one triad minder visible, through a side door, reading a newspaper. I couldn't see Lily, but she'd hardly be allowed to hang around the reception.

The girls were all pretty and fuckable, like a good brothel should be.

The booking lady, looking like a Macau matron, sat me in a leather armchair.

'Me show you girls. You choose which one you like to take upstairs.'

'Sounds good to me, Mama. I'd like to see all the girls, please. I like a lot of choice, including any special girls. And I'm in the mood to spend a lot of money.'

I pulled out a money clip from my jacket pocket, loaded with a phalanx of folded fifties. I called it my bordello billfold. It spoke volumes in these milieus.

Madame Butterfly cooed. 'Ooh, you in for very good time, mister.'

'That's what I came here for, Mama.'

And that, of course, was my problem. Right now, looking at these hot Eastern girls, I was hankering to get laid. But giving Lily a quick shafting before I let her rescuers in was not an option. She was Mr H's daughter. If he got wind I'd touched his girl, I'd become fish food for those motherfucker koi at the Chinese Gardens. This was a real dilemma, a harsh test of my resolve.

Plus, I wasn't about to screw a girl who was being held captive.

As lecherous and debauched as I am, consent is always a red line.

The nubile parade got going. One petite girl particularly took my fancy. She was packing a lot of silicone in her chest. I've always had a thing for petite girls with massive breasts, and I sure wanted to play with those puppies.

'And one more girl, mister. Very exclusive girl.'

She pointed to the doorway where I'd seen the minder. He was now standing behind Lily. She wasn't looking happy. Hardly surprising. But she was a damned fine-looking girl, nothing like her father. She matched the photo I'd been shown, so it was job on.

I felt like a Catholic priest in the altar boys' vestry: frustrated by forbidden possibilities. Not that forbiddance ever saved an altar boy's arse from being sacrificed.

The Kenmare brain was working hard and fast. And then it came to me: a flash of sheer libidinous genius.

'Tell you what, Mama. I'm feeling very excited.' I waved the billfold in front of her again.

Mama looked excited, too.

'I'll take two girls.'

'That expensive, mister.' She smiled. A golden incisor gleamed in her mouth.

'Yep, and I'm paying.'

'Which girls you want?'

'Her,' I said, pointing to the little one who was having trouble balancing with the weight of her tits. 'And her.' I pointed at Lily. 'I like to have someone watch me at work.'

'You do what you like, as long as you pay.' Mama smiled again.

I forked out a shitload of cash and headed off upstairs behind four buttocks that looked more delicious and edible than the finest pork dumplings. Time allowing, I wouldn't have minded pouring sweet and sour sauce all over those two arses and licking their cracks dry. But tonight was a rush job, damn it. Plus Lily was off limits.

A door was closed behind me at the bottom of the stairs. A lock clicked. Yeah, that figured. Looked as if I'd be leaving through the window with Lily.

I was to text a message when I had a window unsecured. Then the Chinese cavalry would arrive, scaling a ladder from the alley below.

Yeah, they could wait a bit.

I took a quick shower in the adjoining bathroom, noting the key lock on the inside of the window. Time for that in due course. I left my clothes hanging on a bathroom chair. Meanwhile, little Miss Big Tits had an appointment with my cock.

Both girls were naked on the bed when I came out. Lily, known here as Jade, was looking surly enough to turn a man gay, but Eve, as the petite one had introduced herself, was smiling and fingering herself. Good girl.

'Okay, Jade, you sit on that chair and watch me and Eve. Then I'll play with you. That's how I like it. Understood?'

She nodded sullenly and got off the bed.

Eve sat up as I got onto the workbench, ran her hands all over me, and rolled a condom onto my raging boner.

I rammed my cock into Eve. Her pussy, surprisingly, was one of the tightest I've ever enjoyed. And those tits! It was like massaging two melon-sized stress-balls.

When I was done, I thanked her and excused myself to go to the toilet. I closed the door and slipped my boxer shorts on.

I got my picklocks out of my jacket and went to work on the window. It was straightforward and I quietly eased it open a couple of centimetres.

I texted 'Go' to the number I had programmed into my phone.

I went back into the bedroom.

'Thanks, Eve, but I want to fuck Jade on her own, so you can go back downstairs. Here's a thank you tip, you were great.' I gave her a hundred and kissed her on the cheek, and not the one I'd envisaged licking sauce off.

She was delighted and left.

Jade was looking extra sullen now. Good job she wasn't in this profession to earn a living. No bloke would want to shag a hooker looking sourer than his mother-in-law.

'Okay, Lily, I know who you are. And I'm not here to have sex with you. We're getting you out of here.'

'What you mean? My name not Lily.'

Now she was looking confused as well as surly.

Before we could continue, I heard noise from the bathroom and suddenly four slim, black-clad, masked figures appeared.

Lily looked scared shitless.

The slimmest of the ninjas, seemingly in charge, said something in Mandarin to Lily. The tone was neither friendly nor respectful. Seemed odd to me.

Lily spoke, in an equally aggressive tone, but her eyes betrayed fear.

The lead ninja issued what must have been a command and two of the others stepped over to Lily. One of them punched her hard in her guts. The other one grabbed her by the hair before she collapsed.

As I said, 'What the fuck?', and moved forward, a Makarov 9mm barrel appeared in my face. The fourth ninja was behind it, two dark eyes glaring ruthlessly at me through the holes in the mask. I reconsidered my chivalry: gun barrels tend to have that effect.

More Mandarin from the boss rescuer, serious punching of Lily, and something verbal from her, but a desperate, pleading tone this time.

The boss pulled out a phone and made a call.

More Chinese chatter, and then a slight pause.

The phone went away and the boss spoke.

One of the men holding Lily produced a boning knife. Without a word, he cut Lily's throat. The other guy let her drop onto the bed, blood spurting from her carotid.

I was going to open my mouth, but the Makarov was still trying to kiss me.

The lead ninja unmasked. A beautiful Chinese lady beamed at me. It was one of those inscrutable looks, exactly like Mr H.

'Mr Kenmare, I am Lily.' She motioned the Makarov down.

'Then who the fuck is she?' I pointed at the butchered whore on the reddening bed.

'She is Lanfen Xu. She worked for my father. She had knowledge of his business, which is why this triad took her. But she also had a code we needed. We got it out of her. I called to make sure the code worked. It did. Then she was no more use and needed to be silenced.'

'Fuck me. Remind me never to get on the wrong side of your old man.'

'You took a while to let us in. Did you have sex with her?'

'No, I screwed another girl first. I didn't touch her because I thought she was you.'

'Very wise man, Mr Kenmare. Now, hold your right hand out.'

'What?'

The Makarov got sleazy again.

'Do it. We are not going to hurt you, you have done your job well.'

'So, why …'

'Just do it, please.'

I complied.

One of the ninja's wrapped my fingers around the handle of the murder weapon. He dropped it in a plastic bag.

Lily was grinning. 'Your fingerprints are our insurance that you will never speak about this matter, Mr Kenmare.'

Not that I would have said jackshit anyway, but they sure had me by the balls. Bloody inscrutable Orientals indeed.

And then it was clothes on and out through the bathroom window.

– 5 –

L ily and her ninjas were all friendly to me once we were in their van and heading back from the job.

Lily handed me her phone during the journey.

Mr H was on the line. 'Thank you, Mr Kenmare, excellent work.'

'No problems, Mr Huang. It's been an interesting assignment.'

I'm sure I heard a chuckle at the other end.

Lily was smirking.

'Lily will pay you. We will keep you in mind for future work.'

'Thank you, Mr Huang.'

He hung up.

I wasn't at all sure about wanting another assignment Mr H-style.

Lily handed me an envelope. It was morbidly obese. I opened it.

'Fuck me!' I heard myself say.

'A healthy bonus for you, Mr Kenmare. We reward professionals who do good work for us. And we believe the only true reward in business is cash.'

'No argument from me. Thank you.'

Yep, okay. I could be up for more of this, Mr H or not.

I got out of the van in Ultimo and waved them goodbye. I took one last look at the exotic and beautiful Lily, decided she'd definitely take charge in bed, and considered what an outrageously fine fuck she'd be. Then I reminded myself only a first-grade retard would even flirt with Mr H's daughter.

I got back to my apartment, drained a much-needed, large Jameson, and got on the phone.

An hour later, my panda girl and friend (and not the panda) had arrived. We were in my bedroom and there wasn't a shred of clothing in sight. As Tom Waits drawled from the stereo about Jersey girls, prostitutes, and kissing lips, Tia rode my face and Imogen rode my cock. Ah, pussy galore.

To borrow from another Australian rogue, 'Such is life.'

* * *

– Case #7 –

THE RELUCTANT BRIDE

Her body was purring at me like a tiger, the proverbial kind of tiger which is dangerous to mount and even more dangerous to dismount.

- Ross Macdonald

THE RELUCTANT BRIDE

– 1 –

She had all the dignity of a novice porn starlet who'd just had the money shot sprayed all over her face, in a gang-bang scene.

I stood there and looked at her, lying back propped up on pillows against the bed-head.

On the one hand, she had this delectable honey-gold skin, high cheek-bones (always up there in my books), tumbling, dark-chestnut locks, smoky-brown eyes, a long, lithe body, and sensational breasts. And, always another point-scorer for me, she was butt naked.

On the other hand, the nakedness was fetid and squalid. Her pubes were a matted mess, semen trails ran down the insides of her thighs, with a hint of shit (at least one of those lads had used the back door), and the room smelt like the inside of a well-patronized wank-tank.

She didn't seem surprised to see another man come through the door of her motel room. Her tongue ventured forth to sweep up a globule of cum on her chin.

Her voice was hoarse. A lot of head in the last hour, I reckoned.

'You want to do me? It's free.' She spread her thighs even further apart.

Being the libertine I am, I would usually have taken her up on her kind offer. However, not this one. Partly because she was the target of my visit, on behalf of my client. But mainly because there was enough jism on and around her to rival the local sperm bank.

And I never swim in another bloke's puddle.

'No thanks, Laila. I came here to *find* you, not fuck you.'

Her wanton look morphed into defiance, like a cornered feline.

'You know my name? Well, tell my parents to go fuck themselves. I'm not part of their family any more. And I'm sure as hell no longer the good little Pakistani virgin they were lining up for my loser cousin back in Lahore.'

'No, it's your sister, Farida, looking for you. She hired me. I'm a private investigator.'

'Oh, I see.'

'But I suspect others are looking as well. You've certainly escaped the family clutches with a bang. And excuse the pun.'

There was a glimmer of a smile. Laila might have woken up a virgin this morning, but she had a naughty streak. Hence why she was here, of course. But her virginity was now a discarded memory, and she wasn't likely to be walking too comfortably for a few days, judging by the look of her red, swollen, dripping crotch.

'I'll still fuck you, detective. A man old enough to be my father will add nicely to all the boys I've just had.'

Those parted thighs, the sodden pussy, the cum trails all over her like a gelatinous road map: no thanks.

'Sorry, I'm working, Laila. And we need to hurry up and get you out of here.'

– 2 –

Ten minutes earlier, I had been standing on the first-floor balcony opposite. It was a typical U-shaped motel, moulded around its potholed car park. And every bit a rooms-by-the-hour establishment. About the only guests who'd stay the whole night would be those who shot up and passed out. Or those on the run.

I knew the manager, Ricky, from a previous job, and had greased his palm sufficiently. Everyone has a price. And now I had a key card to Room 237. Ricky had told me she was in there, checked in this morning. He grinned as he told me some young lads had trooped in there about two hours ago.

'Party girl I reckon, Harry. Mind you, bloody good sort, too. Pure brown sugar, mate.'

And now I watched the boys of the moment parade out of the room like returning victors. Seven of them, all cock-a-hoop and doing high-fives in voluble spirit as they left. Two of them were busy on their phones. Laila Khan's sexual initiation was going to go viral, no doubt. Seven studs with seven loads for one sinful sister.

I waited for the testosterone platoon to get into their two expensive German SUVs and drive away, no doubt back to their respectable, expensive suburbs.

I moved along the balcony until I reached 237. There was a plastic cup on the concrete floor outside, two thirds full of water. Three white cigarette butts circled with magenta lipstick floated in the sepia liquid. The colour was a perfect match to the bougainvillea bushes in full bloom around the car park. The only remotely attractive part of the property.

I slid my ill-gotten key card into the slot and pushed the door open.

– 3 –

Shortly after lunch, I'd been sitting in the Newtown office of Farida Khan, an up-and-coming human rights lawyer, and older sister of Laila.

'Ms Khan, pleased to meet you. Harry Kenmare, PI, at your service.'

'Thank you for coming so quickly, Mr Kenmare.'

'You said it was urgent. And it's Harry, please.'

'Cool. I'm Farida. I need you to find my younger sister, Laila.'

'How old is she?'

'Twenty.'

'So, maybe she doesn't want to be found.'

'Probably not, but best for me to find her before her brothers do.'

Interesting. 'You said "her" brothers, not "our" brothers?'

'I've disowned my conservative family and their backward religion. They follow a twisted version of Islam that adheres to forced marriages and honour killings. You would have read stories over time?'

'Yes, of course.'

'Well, I ran away when I was eighteen. Never looked back. Ten years on, I'm a free and happy atheist.'

'And a considerable human rights lawyer already. I did some quick research after your call.'

I always rate giving compliments to ladies.

'Thank you.'

A smart lawyer who was gracious as well as beautiful. I was liking this assignment.

'I can't think of a more important area of law to work in. I love it, passionately, despite the tragic cases

I deal with. And often lose, given our fascist-leaning governments in Canberra, of both political colours.'

Oh, I seriously liked this lady. I smiled at her. 'And despite my being an ex-detective, I could not agree with you more.'

'You are quite the charmer, aren't you, Harry?'

'I have my moments. And I'm not trying to blow hot air up your shirt, but I very much admire you. The world needs more people with conviction and decency.'

Mind you, I wouldn't have said 'no' to blowing a whole lot of air up all sorts of her places. She was a stunning woman, and I wouldn't be able to resist. But I didn't think that was going to be on the table. Or any other horizontal surface for that matter. No, despite my charm, Farida was probably way out of my league. Alas, back to business.

'Okay, so what's the go with Laila?'

'They had her wedding arranged. Some distant cousin in Pakistan that she'd never met. So fucking primitive!'

She took a deep breath.

'Sorry, I get angry. Anyway, they were keeping a tight leash on Laila, having learnt from my escape. But somehow Laila did get out and she ran for it. I got a text to say she was going to get herself a room, get laid, and put it out on social media so they wouldn't want her anymore.'

'Is it that simple? Escaping?'

'No. They will kill her instead. She copied her parents and brothers into the text. Even by running she has sullied the family honour. They would consider killing her for that alone. But it's definitely death if she has sex.'

'So, what did *you* do when you escaped, if you don't mind me asking?'

She smiled. It was like a sunrise over an exotic landscape. 'They hadn't arranged my marriage yet, so the honour issue wasn't the same. Plus I didn't announce plans for losing my virginity. Laila's done that for maximum effect, but she doesn't take the honour killing seriously.'

'Did you do anything for effect?'

She laughed now. 'I had a plate of bacon and eggs, lots of extra bacon, and washed down with a bottle of red wine. Posted it on social media with my speech of defiance. Got several thousand likes on Twitter in the first twenty-four hours. And a message from father telling me to never, ever come near the family again. He told me I was dead to them.'

I liked this lady's style. 'Good for you. Now, do we have any leads on where Laila might have gone to?'

'Just that she said she was getting a room and getting laid.'

'Has she got any money of her own?'

'Not much, I wouldn't think. You've no idea how controlling some Muslim men can be.'

'I can guess, and it's not restricted to Muslims, I can assure you.'

'Yeah. I steer clear of them, regardless of what type.'

I looked at her aquiline face, her treacle-coloured skin, her large, dark-brown eyes. I tried not to let my gaze drop lower, but I must have slipped. Well, I'm only human. She caught that and looked straight into my eyes. Was there a hint of a smirk there? Or was it my wishful thinking? True to form, I was doing plenty of that, of the most lustful variety.

After a smouldering pause, she said, 'I generally stick to women.'

Her eyes didn't even flicker. Fuck, no wonder she was such a good lawyer. She was playing with me, poker-faced. I took a chance, let the mongrel Kenmare charm out of its kennel.

'Well, my tongue does a rather sensational impersonation of a lesbian.'

She chuckled.

'Is that right?' she said, a slight grin now.

'Never had any complaints. At least not on that front. And I usually get a return invite.'

'Ooh, we are confident, aren't we?'

'Need to be in present company.'

'Ah, touché. But we can resume this banter later, Harry. Laila has to be found, and fast.'

I mentally slapped myself back into action mode.

'So, money. How much would she be likely to have?'

'Not much cash. But she has got a credit card.'

'What? They let her have that?'

'Hell no. I gave it to her. It's very hush-hush. I wanted her to have it for emergencies.'

She looked down for a moment.

'But her getting a hotel room and losing her virginity wasn't exactly what I had in mind.'

'Well, we often don't get to choose our emergencies, although she seems to be the architect of this one. At least today's episode.'

'I don't actually care about her wanting to have sex, that's her life. But I am really scared her brothers will get to her.'

'So, Farida, do you have access to the credit account?'

'Yes, why … Oh, of course. Sorry. Despite my sparring with you, I'm not quite on my game this morning. It's the worry. So, we'll see if she's used it yet?'

'Exactly.'

She turned her laptop so we could both see the screen and her long fingers deftly slid over the keys. I'd never considered I'd find fingers typing to be awash in eroticism, but Farida's were.

'Nothing spent,' she said, looking at the Amex screen.

'Okay, switch to the pending transaction view.'

She clicked. 'Bingo. That one's today. But it's a company name, Southern Chain PL. How does that help?'

'That's why you called me.' I pulled out my phone and pressed a contact.

'Trev? Mate, can you please get on to that corporate database you've got access to?'

'Sure, Harry. What do you need?'

'Mate, Southern Chain PL. Need a trading name and address. Reckon it'll be a hotel or motel.'

'Roger, brother. Bear with me.'

I could hear Trev clacking on his keyboard back in our office.

I looked at Farida whilst I waited. The simmering eyes that were appraising me sure didn't seem exclusively lesbian. Hope sprang eternal in the Kenmare crotch.

'Got it, Harry. Trading name is Centenary Motor Lodge, on Parramatta Road.'

'Shit, that sounds familiar.'

'Yes, mate. It was the one we tailed that real estate agent to. The one who was banging his receptionist.'

I laughed. 'Oh, yes. Will never forget that one.'

I recalled that sweltering afternoon ten months ago. One of Sydney's big-shot real estate agents been a little indiscreet. The wife got suspicious, needed professional help. Enter Kenmare and Associates. And not the only entering that went on that hot day last summer.

Having paid off the motel manager handsomely, Trev and I entered the room of the tryst-*du-jour*, right in time to capture a glorious photo of a naked middle-aged Mister 'Smith'. Said gentleman was tied to the bed, a gag ball in his mouth, with his twenty-year-old receptionist wearing only a nurse's cap with a stethoscope around her neck, and easing her fist into the big man's anus. It was a new variant on the enema game, but the photos we gave to Missus 'Smith' were priceless. She thought so, too, and the bonus we got was considerable. There were some days I seriously loved my work.

I rang off from Trev.

'Righto. I'll get myself to the motel and persuade your young sister to accompany me back here. Does that work?'

'Yes, for now. Then I'll have to think of somewhere to put her, because they'll be hunting her and they know where I live. I don't want them hanging around my place.'

'I can probably assist there. I've got a lot of contacts.'

'Thank you, Harry. Now, please get to her before they do.'

I left her office on King Street and jumped straight in a cab.

– 4 –

Laila had now accepted I wasn't going to add my seed to the seminal swill inside her. I suggested a shower before we got going. She'd had more cock in her in the last hour than most girls did in a year, leaving aside the ladies of the night. She agreed to the wash, although not before taking some awful photos of herself to complete her debasement and exit from the misogynistic world of Muslim forced marriages. The quick video clip she did of her fingers scooping jism from her pussy and licking them clean was front runner for the *pièce de résistance*.

Ten minutes later, she'd washed and dressed, although I swear she still smelt of semen. Or maybe it was the rancid air in the room. I bundled her and her suitcase down to the reception, settled her bill, and slipped Ricky some extra cash.

'She was never, ever here. Okay, Ricky?'

'You can rely on me, Harry.' He slid the fifties into his jeans pocket.

We headed for Farida's office.

– 5 –

I left Laila with Farida, closing the door on animated voices.

I called a contact in the sex industry, Sandrine, the Tunisian temptress. The one night she'd allowed me to get more than professional was one of the most singularly memorable nocturnal sojourns of my entire life.

And it has some stiff competition. I do like the ladies, after all.

Sandrine answered on the third ring.

'Harry, my Celtic charmer. How are we *aujourd'hui*?'

Hell, I loved it when she slipped a French word into that sexy accent.

As much as I love the English language, the French make the spoken word erotic like no others.

'Ah, Miss Carthage of my Mediterranean dreams. I'm well, thanks. And your beautiful self?'

'Wonderful, Harry, *comme toujours*. And to what do I owe the *plaisir*?'

Damn, the French words were making me bar up.

'Oh, babe, if only.'

There was that husky laugh. 'Patience, *mon ch*éri, we will have another liaison.'

'And not soon enough, *ma ch*érie. Anyway, sadly this is a work call.'

'How can I help, handsome?'

'I've got a girl who needs hiding. My client will pay well. Any room in that safe house at the moment?'

'For you, of course. Is she a sex worker?'

My mind flashed back to the cum-covered Laila. 'Not exactly, let me explain.'

I filled her in. We arranged for Laila to stay at the safe house as long as needed.

I called Trev to come and do the taxi run for me.

He arrived in his VW van full of the tools of our trade. Within twenty minutes he had a transmitting camera nestled discreetly in the corner of Farida's office on a bookcase, and he'd loaded a tracking app onto Laila's mobile phone.

– 6 –

After Laila had gone, I sat in Farida's office with her, wondering how I was going to get this lady to stray and permit me to sample her pleasures.

More important, however, was her safety.

'Farida, if your brothers are as fanatical as you say, they're going to keep going until they get Laila. And if they don't know where she is, then they will probably start via you.'

'Possibly, but if she's not at my place, there's not much they can do.'

'Well, you were the one who told me how hard-core they are on their Sharia law. And combined with what

I've read about extreme Islam, I'd say they won't stop at anything. When a severely perverse view of the world overcomes reason, then all common sense bets are off. You should know that better than most, Farida, with respect.'

She rolled her eyes. 'Yes, Harry, thanks for the little pep talk. I agree with what you're saying, but I guess I'm just having a little adjustment problem to my new situation.'

'And fair enough. But part of my job is to do a risk assessment. And right now, I reckon we're at almost certain with extreme consequences.'

'All right. But I'm not about to rearrange my whole life for these arseholes.'

'So, what precautions are you going to take?'

'Nothing extra. To quote one of my heroes, "Equality is the soul of liberty. There is no liberty without it." That perfectly sums up my view, Harry. And no fucking misogynistic, Muslim arsehole is going to take that from me. Even my ex-brothers.'

I nodded in silent admiration at her stand for rights and freedom. We were cousins on that level. I didn't know the quote she'd used.

'Not familiar with your hero there, but love the sentiment.'

She looked intensely at me. 'Frances Wright. A nineteenth century feminist and utopian. She opposed any organized religion and was an advocate of sexual freedom.'

'Cool. I can dig that. Must read some of her work.'

Farida reached behind her to a small bookcase and pulled out a well-worn paperback. 'Here you go, Harry. Broaden your already liberal mind.'

'Don't mind if I do. Always happy to read more.' I turned the book over in my hand.

'Now, about your security, Ms Khan? Apart from the camera that's now in here, I mean.'

'The gallant knight protecting the needy damsel is a bit of a cliché, don't you think?'

'Yeah, probably. But so are self-entitled bastards victimizing women. I know what bad men are capable of.'

'Thanks, and so do I. I've got good security on my place, and when I'm not reading feminist literature for pleasure, or enjoying a fellow feminist for pleasure, I do martial arts.'

'Ouch.' I smiled at her. 'Well, at least agree to call me if you have any concerns. Please?'

'Should I make you beg?'

'Can I choose what I beg for?'

She laughed. 'I'm not turned on by chivalry, I'm afraid. Although I do respect your motivation. Now, if you were sitting there with breasts and a vagina, I might be getting aroused. But, alas …'

'More's the pity. I guarantee my tongue would be worth the deviation.'

'Mmm …' She gazed at me. 'I'll have a think about that.'

'So, where there's life, there's hope?'

'You never know. I don't regard sexuality as strictly binary, and I'm not from the man-hating brigade. But if it happens, it'll be entirely on my terms.'

'Of course. I would expect nothing less. I'll buy a lottery ticket on my way home.'

She laughed again, pure sensuality. She wrote a number on the back of a business card and handed it to me. 'That's not an invitation, by the way. It's just so you've got it for an emergency.'

I looked at her.

'And you feeling randy, Mister, does not count as an emergency.'

She was playing with me again.

We said our farewells and I, as horny as Casanova, wandered out onto King Street for the second time that afternoon.

The pub? Shortly. First I needed some urgent release. Farida had said my need to get laid didn't count as an emergency. She was wrong.

My genital GPS reminded me one of my favourite bordellos, Cum Hither, was a short walk.

I almost ran.

– 7 –

Later that evening, I was at the Emerald Bar, nursing a large Jameson on ice and a sore cock. I think it needed to be on ice, too. The young Russian lady at the parlour had been dynamite.

Katya hadn't spoken too much English, but she moaned convincingly as she rode my cock. Universal language, that one. Hell, I moaned, too, when I exploded. I needed the release big time.

Young Katya's lack of the local lingo didn't interfere with her understanding of another universal language: cash. A large wad of it had me staying on for a second round, once she got me aroused again. This time I went doggy, hanging on to her magnificent breasts hanging pendulously beneath her. Well, as pendulous as silicone gets, anyway. An even larger wad of fifties got me another hour. She suggested, mainly with her fingers, I might like to venture round back to the tradesman's entrance. At least, Russian not being on my skills list, that's how

I interpreted her licking her finger and sticking it in her arse. Her other fingers also assisted with counting out the fifties. It was an expensive brothel visit, but going for my third foray, this time into Katya's enticing anus, was worth every cent.

Over my whiskey, I was perusing social media (an area I was reluctantly coming to grips with) on my iPhone to see if I could find young Laila in her hour of cum-sodden glory. Given her age group, I'd gone for Instagram to start with, but although I found her page, there was nothing salacious on it. Not so surprising, given the censorious attitude of Facebook and its subsidiaries: more favourable to dishonest politicians and their propaganda than good old-fashioned porn.

No, Twitter was the jackpot. She'd loaded some short video clips and hashtagged them '#sluttypakivirgin'. No wonder it was trending. But it also led me directly to the various videos the young men had loaded up.

What a fuckfest!

As I trawled, I saw the usual lascivious contributions, mostly guys wanting more from her, but then I got to the nastier stuff. A couple of presumably random, Muslim douchebags slagging her off. Those guys were no doubt screwing around at will, but for a Muslim woman to do it was a heinous crime. I've never been able to stomach hypocritical wankers, especially the ever-plentiful religious ones.

I spotted one of Laila's brothers, Bilal: 'You gonna die, bitch, Sharia style.'

Next the other brother, Afraz, chiming in: 'You gonna be stoned, you slut.'

I guessed he wasn't referring to a session on the weed.

And then a whole load of good, pious, Muslim boys were piling in on top. For supposedly decent religious people, they had a solid vocabulary for abusing women in the basest way. No wonder Farida had been so worried.

I took a slug of my Jameson, and lamented the state of the world. What some of these pricks needed was some good old-fashioned policing, not this politically correct, soft-cock, social-work approach that now dressed itself in a blue uniform. The bloody cops were either too busy pussy-footing around so they didn't upset anyone, or they were being used as political enforcers by the increasingly authoritarian governments around Australia. The lucky country? Like hell it was. Fuck it. More whiskey was needed.

Jameson, a great panacea, I find: fixes most despondency. That or sex. Yeah, my doctor and I don't agree on much. *C'est la vie!*

I raised my empty glass and the barmaid came over and smiled. She was a new girl: Spanish it turned out, here on a gap year. I considered turning on the Kenmare charm, offering to help her fill a gap or three. No, sadly, a raincheck was in order as my cock was way too worn and exhausted thanks to Katya. So, señorita Lucia would have to wait. Not that she knew it yet. Well, at least in my fantasies. No harm there.

– 8 –

The phone woke me. Through a half-opened eye, I glanced at the clock radio: 4.15 a.m. I normally flick the phone to silent at night, but the old gut feeling had been twitching yesterday.

I fought myself awake through the Jameson fumes and picked up the insistent beast.

It was Farida.

'Farida, you okay?'

'Don't know. Had some really violent messages left on my voicemail. And now there are noises around the back yard.'

'Have you called the cops?'

'Yes, but not much use, Harry. The local cops don't have any time for me after I represented the family of that indigenous kid who died in the cells last year. They said they'd get a patrol car to swing past when one was free, but I could hear them laughing in the background.'

'All right. Myself and a mate will get there as soon as we can.'

'Thanks, Harry.'

I hung up and called Trev. I'd put him on stand-by, the old gut feeling and all.

'Be there in five or so, Harry. Meet you on the street.'

'Roger that. And tool up, Trev.'

'No worries, brother.'

We made it to Farida's street in Redfern, the gentrified section, in under fifteen minutes from her call. We did a drive along Great Buckingham Street past the front of her house, but nothing doing. We pulled over in a side street and got out to head up Castlereagh Lane behind the houses.

Trev and I stepped into the dark laneway, gats discreetly ready by our legs. The air was that pre-dawn cool and moist. Brought back memories of night shift in the cops. No matter how much sleep you'd had during the day, you were still nodding off in the patrol van about 4 a.m. Circadian rhythms I'd read somewhere. A similar time on the clock also brought back memories of furtively departing various one-night-stand hostesses.

I could make out Farida's place from the back as she'd put lights on, although the lane was still dark. The street light at the far end was on, but the other two unlit along the lane obviously hadn't made it onto the city council's to-do list yet. No doubt more important things to spend the ratepayers' money on, such as the Lord Mayor's annual ball, and not to forget the growing collection of dog-ugly artworks in public spaces.

We walked down either side of the alley, manoeuvring around the assorted garbage bins.

I saw Trev moving towards me out of the corner of my eye.

'There's someone behind the telegraph pole at her back fence,' he whispered.

Sure enough, there was a rounded shape not completely obscured by the pole. Made it look like a pregnant beanstalk.

At that moment, there was a flash of movement as another figure came out of Farida's back garden over the top of the fence.

We both broke into a run, but the noise of our feet slapping on the bitumen broke the quiet and alerted the two miscreants. One of them called something in a foreign lingo and they took off sprinting.

We followed suit, but as we drew close to Farida's back fence, a third figure clambered over the top, dropping into the laneway in a crouch, and meeting my heel as I launched it into his face.

Trev sank his toecap into the night prowler's groin.

I looked at the two diminishing human shapes at the end of the lane. 'We'll just give this fuck the message, brother, I can't be arsed chasing the others.'

'Jeez, he fucking stinks, mate.' Trev kicked him again. 'Ever take a shower, cunty?'

As I leant down to grab the bloke by his throat, the stench of rancid lamb fat and curry spices, competing with BO, nearly asphyxiated me. 'Let's have some light, partner.'

Trev flicked on a pocket Maglite and I watched the cousin, Uday, squint his eyes closed.

'Open your eyes, cunt. Want you to see this coming.'

Two slits appeared. 'Fuck you' followed.

I felt his nose break as I drove my fist into his face. It felt good, damned good.

I love taking down bullies.

'Now listen, fucktard, and listen good. You go near Farida or Laila and we're going to kill you.'

He spluttered a bit with the blood running out of his nose into his mouth. 'We will deliver Allah's will, so fuck you infidels.'

'Mate, I really don't think he's listening,' said Trev.

'No, clearly needs more pain.' I looked around in the shadows and spotted my tool of improvisation: a house brick lying next to the wooden pole.

'Hold him down, brother.'

'Roger that, my pleasure.' Trev put his foot on Uday's throat.

I picked up the brick and drove its corner into the arsehole's right kneecap. He would have screamed like a banshee, were it not for Trev's foot restricting his air supply. Even so, the muted howl of agony was heart-warming for a man of justice.

Scum need to feel pain: it's all they understand, and they sure inflict enough of it in the world.

I gestured to Trev to release his foot pressure.

'Now, Uday, do we understand each other? You don't touch Laila or Farida.'

He looked into my eyes, still squinting in the torchlight beam. Despite the pain he was in, I could see defiance and loathing seething in those eyeballs.

That's religious zealots for you, regardless of creed.

'Think he's still short on understanding, mate,' said Trev.

'Yeah, another lesson required.'

I pinned Uday's right forearm to the bitumen, and slammed the brick into his hand. I heard the crunch as various bones broke. The scream this time was louder, without the constricted windpipe. It was piercing enough to potentially draw the attention of any early risers in the houses overlooking. I did his other hand for good measure.

I leant over, trying not to breathe through my nose: the stench from this arsehole was foul.

'So, listen good, cunty. If we ever see you again, or hear that you or your wanker Muslim mates have been anywhere near the girls, we will hunt you down and you'll be dead meat. And I'll be sure to butcher you halal-style. Just to keep your bloody Allah friend happy.'

Trev sniggered. 'Nice touch, mate. Now let's fuck off.'

'Roger that.' I sank my toecap into Uday's ribs, and Trev followed suit. We legged it back up the laneway, and into the van and away.

'I don't think we've seen the last of that lot, Harry.'

'No, mate. As sure as a lying politician. Only these cunts are more dangerous.'

'Yep, we're going to need to be ready. I can feel it in my gut.'

'Mine too. Now, talking of guts, let's go and get a feed of bacon and eggs.'

'With some good pork sausages.

178

'I'm salivating already.'

Trev chuckled. 'And all halal, of course.'

I laughed, too. 'Absolutely, *habibi*.'

I called Farida to let her know the threat was gone.

For now.

– 9 –

Hours later, I was half-asleep in my armchair with a bellyful of cooked breakfast, and thinking about that hot Russian hooker. I had one of those dreamy semi-erections. Trev was stretched out on the couch, snoring lightly.

My reverie was broken by the alarm tone from Trev's phone: not the clock, but the special app he'd installed to connect with Farida's office.

Trev came alive immediately: years of professional practice.

'Let's move it. You drive, Harry. I'll get the video feed up.'

'Roger that.' I grabbed the van keys on the hall-stand, Trev grabbed his laptop, and we bolted for the lift down to the car park.

We made record time getting onto the road to head for Newtown.

'I reckon traffic will be a bitch up King Street, mate.'

'Let's just make sure we don't get pulled over, Harry. Don't need some nosey copper looking too closely in the van.'

'Hell no.'

'Okay, the feed's live. Shit, the girl can fight. There's three of them in there, although one's got bandaged hands and isn't doing much.'

'Fuck!' I jammed on the brakes as a light went red.

I looked over at the laptop screen. Farida obviously did know some sort of martial art, because she was kicking and punching as if her life depended on it. It likely did.

'Shit, she's good, mate.'

'Not wrong, Harry. I'd always want her on my side.'

A horn blasted behind us. I looked up to a green light and planted my foot. I amber-gambled at the next traffic lights, hurling the van left onto City Road. I stuck to the speed limit, reluctantly, hoping for a reasonably clear run.

'Mate, she's hammering them. Our fucktard friend from the alleyway has already limped out and she's laying some great kicks on the other two. They both look beat.'

Another bloody red light. I looked back at the screen in time to see the last of the thugs hauling his flogged arse out of the office door.

As we pulled up in a loading zone short of the office front on King Street, I saw one of the brothers scooting around the corner into a side street.

The priority, however, was to check on Farida, although it seemed from the footage that she'd certainly looked after herself. We raced inside.

'Ah, the tardy cavalry,' said Farida, grinning. She had a sexy, sweaty sheen over her face and neck.

'Nice work, we were watching,' said Trev.

'When I escaped the family, I knew defending myself would be a vital asset, so I took up taekwondo. Now I'm a black belt first dan.'

She pointed to a photo and certificate on the wall, next to her law degree and law master's. I hadn't noticed it on my previous visits.

'Do you think there's any likelihood of them coming back?' I asked.

'No. They got nothing out of me, other than the humiliation of being beaten by a woman.'

Trev laughed. 'Yep, a great whipping. Love your work.'

She smirked. 'I need a drink after that. Why don't we get some lunch at the pub down the road?'

'Damned fine idea. My shout,' I said.

'I should bloody well hope so,' she said, 'after I've done all the heavy lifting around here!'

– 10 –

We'd finished an excellent steak at the Bear Hotel, I'd reluctantly swapped to lime and soda due to having to drive the van home, and Trev was making eyes at a couple of the staff. It was a predominantly gay pub. Trev assured me he'd sampled the dessert menu here before, and it was greatly to his taste. Well, good on him. After all, we're here for a good time, not a long time.

Farida joined in, polishing off the side serve of bacon she'd had with her steak. 'I stick it to Islam every chance I get.' She smiled mischievously, and went on to brag that she'd pulled some excellent sex in here as well.

Not my joint, obviously. The only thing I'd be pulling in here, voluntarily at least, was my own dick.

'Okay, you two, whilst you're both organizing your next root, I'll stay on the job and check in on Laila.'

Farida dragged her eyes from a well-toned, crew-cut woman across the room to look at me. 'Good, Harry, because I'm currently paying you. Plus I don't think you're going to get lucky in here. Unless you're flexible on your team membership?'

'No, babe. Many things in my life have been a total fuck-up, but my sexuality has always been a dead cert.'

She smirked, looked at me longer than necessary (damn, she got movement in me every time) and turned back to the lesbian across the room.

I got on the phone to the safe house.

It didn't sound good. I hung up.

'Guys, we might have a problem,' I announced.

The other two minds at the table came out of respective bedrooms and focused on me.

'Laila's gone.'

'What?' Farida had alarm in her eyes.

'Told the safe house manager that she had a message from her cousin, Mina. Cousin wanted to meet to see if she could help her.'

'Oh, fuck,' said Farida, heads turning to look at her. 'Mina is the original poster girl Muslim. Wears the whole burka even.'

'A trap?' asked Trev.

'It must be. Mina's only idea of helping someone would be to give Osama Bin Laden a blow-job.'

'Trev, fire up that tracking app on Laila's phone and we'd better move.'

'Can I come?' asked Farida.

'No!' replied Trev and I in one noise.

'It's likely to get ugly, babe,' I said.

'And probably illegal,' added Trev.

'We'll keep you posted. Leave you to go and introduce yourself to that lady over there, if you're still in the mood, that is.'

She nodded, a glint in her eye, and looked at me. 'I'll grab her number, but the rest of the mood's gone. I want to know Laila is safe first.'

'Understandable, and we will do our best. And don't forget the lesbian credentials of the Harry Kenmare tongue. Yours anytime. Just saying.'

She smiled. And again looked longer than required. 'Find Laila for me.'

Trev and I scooted out to the van.

– 11 –

We located the phone-tracker signal heading towards the west of the city. It was moving at a rate of knots, so Laila was in a vehicle.

'We won't know what car,' said Trev. 'But we can follow the signal. Will keep us close, anyhow.'

'Best bet we've got.'

'Okay, Harry, it's turning onto Canterbury Road, so my bet is heading for the Bankstown or Lakemba area.'

'Fucking hell. One minute we've got her safe and sound in a refuge with battered hookers. Now she's on her way to some extreme Muslim hell.'

'Guessing that's where we come in, brother.'

'Yeah, I know, but I don't fancy the two of us trying to storm some Islamic fortress in Lakemba. It's like the shitty, Hezbollah end of Beirut these days. Don't think the numbers would be in our favour.'

'Nothing would be in our favour, mate. We're both screaming atheists, both ex-detectives, plus I'm gay. Some of those fucks throw people like me off the top of tall buildings.'

'Yeah, primitive scum. But we need a plan, or that girl is going to die. And it'll be a horrible death.'

'So, let's see where she goes.'

Fifteen minutes later, we were in central Lakemba and the signal stopped. We'd been following one solitary vehicle, a tinted-window Audi SUV, for the last three streets, so logic said Laila, or at least her phone, was in that car.

The Audi pulled into a driveway of a gated, kitsch-looking, three-storey house. The typical ugly architecture of certain Middle-Eastern immigrants, eager to flash their wealth, often obtained through crime or corruption. All ostentation, and zero class.

A garage door slithered up and the dark SUV slid inside.

'Fuck, what now?'

'Wait and see, at least for a bit, mate,' said Trev. 'We can't exactly launch an assault on that mansion. I'll do a bit of digging online.'

I lit a smoke, lowering the window. I gave Trev one as well, and he drew back as he tapped away on his trusty keyboard. In this day and age I depended on having a tech-savvy partner.

'Okay, Harry, this address belongs to an imam, Yoosuf Al-Mehdi. He's one of those extreme types. Suspected links to al-Qaeda. Been pulled in by the Feds for questioning. Nothing's ever stuck.'

'Fucking swell, just what we need. Mind you, they're not likely to do anything to her in the imam's place. He wouldn't want dirt directly on his hands.'

'True. Maybe they're going to get some sort of permission or sanction authorized.'

'Yeah, that makes sense. Let's watch their social media feeds, Trev.'

'On it, brother.'

Nothing happened for over three hours. The sun set and Sydney was enveloped in darkness. I was half-asleep sitting behind the wheel of our van. Trev was playing on his laptop.

There was a beep.

'Shit, phone's moving,' said Trev. 'And quickly. She's mobile again.'

'But that SUV hasn't come back out.'

'They must have switched cars and left via a different exit. We can follow close enough with the tracker. They're heading north, let's move.'

I started the van and we took off in pursuit.

– 12 –

Fifty minutes later, we were approaching Hornsby.
'Signal's stopped moving,' said Trev. 'From the map, it looks like the disused quarry.'

'Perfect location for whatever atrocity they've got in mind for Laila.'

'Yeah, but also perfect for a pair of vigilantes like us, brother.'

'Roger that. Which way?'

'Turn right down here. It's the approach road into the quarry, so maybe kill the lights and take it real slow.'

I kept the van in first gear and in the middle of the gravel road. There were shrubs and trees on both sides of the track, until we rounded a bend and it was suddenly clear on the right-hand side, with a view to the old workings below. In the moonlight, I could see the floor of the quarry, now mostly flooded pits, with an area of dry ground remaining near the rusting machinery sheds. Car headlights illuminated four figures, one surrounded by the other three.

'There they are, Trev. She's still alive.'

I pulled over on the other side of the track to keep our vehicle out of sight. We silently exited the van and stepped over to the edge to look down on the quarry. It was like looking into the abyss of some medieval, religious hell.

Laila yelling 'Fuck you!' was clearly audible amongst the noises of the nocturnal wildlife.

I whispered to Trev, 'If we barrel on in, they'll probably kill her before we can get there.'

One of the men punched Laila in the guts and she dropped to her knees.

'Yep, you're right, Harry. So, fancy the sniper rifle?'

'Fuck, they're picking up rocks. They *are* going to stone her.'

'Barbaric cunts,' said Trev as he ran back to the van.

As the first stones hit Laila, still on her knees, Trev flicked open the bipod on the stock of a Sako .223 rifle with nightscope, handing it to me.

'You're the better shot, brother.'

True, I always beat Trev at the firing range.

I crouched behind a boulder and positioned the weapon. I actioned the bolt and a brass shell with its high-velocity slug of death slid into the chamber.

Always love that sound and feel.

I focused the scope on the head of Bilal, who was raising his arm with another rock in his hand.

Breath held. Gentle, even squeeze of the finger.

CRACK!

I watched through the scope as the side of the arsehole's head sprayed over a shed wall behind him.

The other two devout wankers turned in our direction, looking like stunned possums.

Which one next?

The decision was made by a blade appearing from the belt of the cousin, Uday.

CRACK!

The back of his head showered over the ground, and the corpse of the dead Bilal.

The remaining brother, Afraz, looked around helplessly. His last act of primeval fanaticism was to run towards Laila, a machete now in his hand.

A moving target was harder.

CRACK!

The first slug hit him in the shoulder, spinning him around.

CRACK!

My second round ripped through his neck and he dropped, two metres from Laila, now huddled on the ground.

'Nice work, Harry,' said Trev, lowering his binoculars. 'You haven't lost your touch.'

'Three fewer scum in the world. Anyway, they were probably going to end up suicide bombers or some other stellar career choice. We've done the world a favour, as well as Laila.'

'Let's go get her.'

Headlights on now, we drove down to the quarry floor as quickly as the dodgy track would allow, stopping next to the carnage.

Laila was moaning on the ground, and bleeding from her hands, head and face. We carried her to the van and put her in the back.'

'Right, let's get rid of them,' I said.

'All in the car, and then swim time, brother. These water-filled quarry pits are deep, real deep.'

'Roger that.'

We put all three dead men into the Mercedes sedan they'd arrived in, closing the doors, but putting the windows down a few centimetres. Handbrake off and transmission in neutral.

Trev jumped in the van and I directed him slowly in reverse until the back bumper of the VW was resting against the back of the Merc. I gave him the thumbs up.

Gently in reverse gear, the van propelled the car towards the edge of the aquatic tomb.

And over it went.

I signalled to Trev to stop. I watched until the last of the car had dropped under the dark surface of the water. Only bubbles were left.

– 13 –

The phone woke me the next morning. Well, just morning: it was nearly twelve. I could hear Trev snoring out on the couch. We'd put in a grand effort on the Jameson after the quarry massacre and getting Laila to hospital, reuniting her with Farida. We'd spared the details, simply assured her Laila wouldn't be bothered again, ever. I'm sure she got the drift, and she was way too smart to want the knowledge, as much as her innate curiosity must have eaten at her.

Lawyers understand exactly what 'accessory after the fact' means.

'Morning, handsome Harry the Hero.' Even her voice motivated my erectile tissue.

'Morning, Farida. How's Laila doing?'

'She'll be fine, given some time. She's pretty bruised, a couple of fractures, but she'll be good after some rest and recuperation. There'll be some permanent scars, but she'll move on.'

'Does she remember the stoning?' Whilst I was genuinely concerned about Laila's welfare and what she might recall of her ordeal, I also had an ulterior motive for asking.

'Just the first couple, until she got hit on the head. She's a blank after that.'

Excellent news. Didn't need her recalling the gunfire and the .223 rounds ripping her mongrel relatives apart.

'Probably best that way,' I said.

'Why don't you and Trev come over for dinner tonight? I can settle up the bill. And decide what bonus to give you for your fantastic work.'

My erection hardened.

'Sounds *delicious*.' I stressed the second word to the point of salaciousness.

'And Trev will be in good company, too.'

'Oh, how so?'

'My intern, Darius, will be joining us. He and Trev were exchanging glances at the office the other day.'

'Really?'

'Yes, really. I notice these things, even if the hotshot PI doesn't.'

'Yeah, funny ha-ha. That sly dog Trev never mentioned anything.'

I recalled the young lawyer with his immaculate appearance and slim-fit suit over a gym-worked body from when we'd installed the camera gear in the office. I'd figured the intern was gay, but I missed Trev's interest.

Farida laughed. 'Be here at seven. Bring wine. Good wine.'

'Of course,' was all I could get in before she rang off.

– 14 –

The excellent Thai banquet and bottles of fine cabernet sauvignon were a distant memory downstairs.

Farida had meant what she said when she'd talked about 'on her terms'.

Harry Kenmare, PI, had met his match. And capitulated, even faster than a British general in 1942 Singapore.

I was tied to the four bedposts with an erection so hard I thought the head of my cock was going to split open.

Farida was astride my face for the second time, only having taken a minute after her first bouncing orgasm on my mouth. She was riding my visage like a rampant rodeo artiste on speed and, boy, could she scream. So, my tongue was going at it harder than a slave rowing in a Roman galley.

Unlike her younger sister's thick, unkempt bush, Farida's pubic mound was trimmed to a small, decorative triangle. Her labia were thick and juicy, and I was loving being almost suffocated in their wetness. I didn't have the option of providing supplementary action with my fingers, so my tongue carried the Kenmare banner as I circled her clitoris and delved in and out of her vulva.

As she bounced on my face more and more vigorously, I felt my nose get banged extra hard and soon tasted blood in the back of my throat. Oh, the wounds of war!

I swallowed a mixture of pussy-infused saliva and blood. Ah yes, way to go.

The increasing noise next door, where Trev and Darius were going at it like a pair of gay bonobos on Viagra, was drowned out as Farida's smooth, muscly, treacle-coloured thighs clamped around my ears, and she screamed as she came again on my face.

Nothing said, she slid downwards and her hand grabbed my rigid and oh-so-ready shaft. And then sheer ecstasy as I eased into paradise, Farida lowering her drenched pussy gradually onto my cock. She rode me. I wasn't going to hold out long: too much desire built up eating her.

'I'm horny as fuck, I'm not going to last.'

She looked down at me. 'I've had two sensational orgasms already, so you take as long or as little time as you want. Either way, you're going to eat me again afterwards.' She grinned.

As I savoured the magnificent feeling of her gliding up and down my rod, I heard Trev reach his moment next door, hollering as he presumably unloaded inside Darius. Strangely, the gay anal adventures going on the other side of the wall didn't interfere with my mood in here. In fact, it seemed listening to Trev shagging Darius was simply heightening the sexual temperature in here. Who would've guessed?

Oh, damn it. I wasn't holding on any longer. I yelled, 'Fuck, yes!' as I blew my load inside Farida.

Another fine assignment completed by Kenmare and Associates, with total customer satisfaction.

Life was good. I wouldn't be dead for quids.

* * *

Epigraph Sources

Case # 1 – Page 1:

1. James Crumley © 1975
   The Wrong Case, p.216. (Edition – Vintage Books 1986).

Case # 2 – Page 25:

2. Ken Bruen © 2002
   The Killing of the Tinkers, p.46. (Edition – Brandon 2010).

Case # 3 – Page 47:

3. Charles Bukowski © 1994
   Pulp, p.4. (Edition – Virgin Books 2009).

Case # 4 – Page 73:

4. Elliott Chaze © 1953
   Black Wings has my Angel, p.194. (Edition – Bruin Books 2011).

Case # 5 – Page 109:

5. Frank De Blase © 2013
    Pine Box for a Pin-up, p.127. (Edition – Down and Out Books 2013).

Case # 6 – Page 133:

6. Kinky Friedman © 1986
    Greenwich Killing Time, p.134. (Edition – Faber and Faber 1997).

Case # 7 – Page 155:

7. Ross Macdonald © 1965
    Black Money, p.99. (Edition – Orion Books 2013).

Glossary

Naturally my writing includes a variety of Australian colloquialisms and other words that may be unfamiliar to overseas readers. As well, law enforcement and its seedy world carries its own slang and jargon, which may well be alien to some readers, both here in Australia and overseas. And there are some foreign language words that appear. Anyway, the following list will hopefully assist.

Australianisms & Colloquialisms (in the sense they are used in this text)

Note: Some are not exclusively Australian, but are included nonetheless as there are significant variations between the various versions of English in the world.

banknote (note)	bank-bill (in the USA)
bareback	sexual intercourse without a condom
bikie	motorcycle gang member ('biker' in the USA)
bonnet (of a car)	hood (in the USA)
boofhead	idiot, stupid person

boot (of a car)	trunk (in the USA)
bush (the)	the Australian outback (countryside)
Canberra	the national (Federal) capital of Australia
claret	blood
colours	(for bikies) the gang logo worn on the leather jackets
Commodore	a very popular, large car made by Holden (GM Australia)
demon	detective
dero	tramp, itinerant
down under	Australia
Feds	Australian Federal Police
gat	handgun
gear	hard drugs (usually heroin)
goanna	native Australian lizard (often large)
good sort	attractive girl or woman
GPS	Global Positioning System (navigational technology)
grog	alcohol
gum tree	eucalyptus tree
hotshot	a deliberately administered lethal overdose of drugs (usually heroin)
klicks	kilometres

kookaburra	native Australian bird with a cackle-sounding noise
KY	lubricant (sexual)
Leb/Lebbo	person of Lebanese origin
minge	vagina
note	see 'banknote'
NSW	New South Wales (the State of)
pavement	sidewalk (in the USA)
ped	paedophile
pineapples	Australian $50 notes (yellow in colour)
piss	alcohol
poofter	(derogatory) male homosexual
Port Botany	the main shipping port for Sydney
Rhodes Scholar	a person gaining the international scholarship to Oxford University
R.M. Williams	an Australian brand of outback clothing and footwear
rock spider	paedophile, child molester
'roger'	(in dialogue) police jargon for 'affirmative', usually used over the police radio
root	sexual intercourse

shag	sexual intercourse
shout	a round of drinks at a bar (noun) / to buy a shout (verb)
State Premier	leader of a state government (equivalent to a State Governor in the USA)
wank-tank	peep show cubicle/venue
windscreen	windshield (in the USA)

Foreign words

aujourd'hui	today (French)
c'est la vie	that's life (French)
chéri (masc.) / *chérie* (fem.)	beloved or darling (French)
comme toujours	as always (French)
du-jour	of the day (French)
habibi	my friend or my love (Arabic)
pièce de résistance	the most remarkable feature (French)
plaisir	pleasure (French)

Acknowledgements

Well, my first book of short stories and the third book I've written and published. I love the authoring life, and one day I'll be able to do it full-time. One should never stop chasing the dream.

Whilst an author writes, largely, in isolation, getting the written word into a published form requires many other contributions, and so I've got plenty of people I wish to thank.

First and foremost, my huge thanks to my partner Ruth for her support, beta reading all the draft stories, and for putting up with my writing stuff spread all over our apartment. I'll make it up to her when I'm a best-selling author!

My thanks to my sister, Katie, and to my friend, Allan Yates, for being beta readers of the drafts, an invaluable role in the whole writing project.

My immense gratitude to those anthology magazine editors in the USA who have liked my short stories enough to publish them: Scotch Rutherford at *Switchblade*, and J. D.

Graves at *Econoclash Review*. Gentlemen, your acceptance of my work has motivated me more than I can express.

And for the professional expertise and services provided during the production stages of the project …

My thanks to J. T. Lindroos, in the USA, for the glorious cover design (I seriously love the cover!). A couple of my own photos feature, including the jacarandas and my local pub, which becomes Harry's Emerald Bar in the stories. J. T. utterly captured the essence of this book.

My thanks to Ran Scott, also in the USA, for the beautifully dark and brooding interior artwork. I stepped outside the box, for a book anyway, with having artwork inside the book, having seen Ran's impressive work in another of my favourite anthology magazines, *Pulp Modern*. So, I sent Ran the draft stories and he produced the stunning images you see inside the book. He nailed it, too.

My thanks to Andy McDermott and his team at Publicious Book Publishing Services, here in Australia, for the book production.

My thanks to my friend Stephen Hill, at Dylunio here in Sydney, for all my other design work, including the logo, stationery, bookmarks, and posters.

Thank you, all!